Presents

Happy New Year! Have you made any resolutions for 2007?

The editors of Harlequin Presents books have made their resolution: to continue doing their very best to bring you the ultimate in emotional excitement every month during the coming year—stories that totally deliver on compelling characters, dramatic story lines, fabulous foreign settings, intense feelings and sizzling sensuality!

January gets us off to a good start with the best selection of international heroes—two Italian playboys, two gorgeous Greek tycoons, a French count, a debonair Brit, a passionate Spaniard and a handsome Aussie. Yummy!

We also have the crème de la crème of authors from around the world: Michelle Reid, Trish Morey, Sarah Morgan, Melanie Milburne, Sara Craven, Margaret Mayo, Helen Brooks and Annie West, who debuts with her very first novel, *A Mistress for the Taking*.

Join us again next month for more of your favorites, including Penny Jordan, Lucy Monroe and Carole Mortimer—seduction and passion are guaranteed!

Bedded by...

Blackmail

Forced to bed...then to wed?

He's got her firmly in his sights and she's got
only one chance of survival—surrender to his
blackmail...and him...in his bed!

Bedded by... **Blackmail**

The *big* miniseries from Harlequin Presents®.

Dare you read it?

Melanie Milburne

BOUGHT FOR THE MARRIAGE BED

Bedded by…

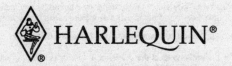

Blackmail

Forced to bed…then to wed?

HARLEQUIN®

TORONTO • NEW YORK • LONDON
AMSTERDAM • PARIS • SYDNEY • HAMBURG
STOCKHOLM • ATHENS • TOKYO • MILAN • MADRID
PRAGUE • WARSAW • BUDAPEST • AUCKLAND

ISBN-13: 978-0-373-12599-9
ISBN-10:   0-373-12599-2

BOUGHT FOR THE MARRIAGE BED

First North American Publication 2007.

Copyright © 2006 by Melanie Milburne.

All about the author...
Melanie Milburne

MELANIE MILBURNE read her first Harlequin novel when she was seventeen and has never looked back. She decided she would settle for nothing less than a tall dark handsome hero as her future husband. Well, she's not only still reading romance, but writing it as well! And as for the tall dark handsome hero, she fell in love with him on the second date and was secretly engaged to him within six weeks!

Two sons later, they arrived in Hobart, Tasmania—the jewel in the Australian crown. Once their boys were in school, Melanie went back to university and received her bachelor's and then master's degree.

For her final assessment, she conducted a tutorial in literary theory concentrating on the romance genre. As she was reading a paragraph from the novel of a prominent Harlequin author, the door suddenly burst open. The husband that she thought was working was actually standing there dressed in a tuxedo, his dark brown eyes centered on her startled blue ones. He strode across the room, hauled Melanie into his arms and kissed her deeply and passionately before setting her back down and leaving without a single word. The lecturer gave Melanie a high distinction and her fellow students gave her jealous glares! And so her pilgrimage into romance writing was set!

Melanie also enjoys long-distance running and is a nationally ranked top-ten master's swimmer in Australia. She learned to swim as an adult, so for anyone who thinks they can't do something—you can! Her motto is "Don't say I can't; say I CAN TRY."

CHAPTER ONE

NINA stared at her twin sister in shock. 'You surely don't mean to go through with it?'

Nadia gave her a defiant look from beneath lashes heavy with thick black mascara. 'I can't cope with a baby. Besides, I never really wanted her in the first place.'

'But Georgia is so young!' Nina protested. 'How can you possibly think of giving her away?'

'It's easy.' Nadia pouted. 'This is a once-in-a-lifetime opportunity. If I don't take it with both hands it might never come again.'

'But she's only four months old!' Nina cried. 'Surely you owe it to Andre's memory to raise her.'

'I owe him nothing!' Nadia spat. 'You seem to be forgetting that he refused to acknowledge her as his child. He wouldn't even agree to a paternity test, no doubt because he didn't want to upset that cow of a fiancée of his.' She paced the room angrily. 'I should've known he wasn't to be trusted. The Marcello males are known for their playboy lifestyle; you have only to look at yesterday's paper to realise that.'

Nina was well aware of the photograph of Marc Marcello, Andre's older brother, in the Sydney weekend broadsheet. It was rare for a week to go past without some reference to his billionaire fast-paced fast-women lifestyle. His dark good looks had been the first thing she'd noticed when she'd opened the paper.

'Does Marc Marcello know about your intention to give his niece up for adoption?' she asked her sister.

Nadia turned back to face her. 'I wrote to his father in Italy a few weeks ago but he flatly refused to acknowledge Georgia as his granddaughter. So this time I sent a photo of her. That should set the cat among the pigeons, when he sees how like Andre she is. I felt the need to twist the knife since it's his precious son's fault my life has been stuffed up.'

'But surely—'

Nadia gave her a bristling look. 'As far as I'm concerned, I want nothing more to do with the Marcello family. I gave them a chance to claim Georgia but they brushed me off. That's why I'm leaving now to get on with Plan B.'

'*Leaving?*' Nina stared at her in consternation. 'Leaving to go where?'

'America.'

'But what about Georgia?' she gasped, her heart tripping in alarm. 'You're surely not thinking of…' She couldn't even frame the rest of the words.

Nadia gave a dismissive shrug of one shoulder. 'You can look after her for a month or two—you do most of the time anyway. Besides, it's clear she loves you more than me, so I don't see why I shouldn't hand her over to you temporarily. You can take care of her until someone adopts her.'

Nina's stomach rolled over painfully. It was hard for her to imagine her sister having so little regard for the tiny infant who lay sleeping in the pram near the window. How could she be so unfeeling as to walk away from her own baby?

'Look—' she tried to reason with her '—I know you're upset; it's only been a few months since Andre…went.'

Nadia turned on her furiously. 'What's with the euphemism? Andre didn't *go* somewhere—he *died*.'

Nina swallowed. 'I—I know.'

'I'm just glad he took his stupid fiancée with him,' Nadia added in a surly tone.

'You surely don't mean that?'

Nadia's features twisted in bitterness. 'Of course I mean it. I hate the Marcello family and anyone connected to them.' She tossed her mane of blonde hair over one shoulder and looked back at her sister. 'I have a chance at a new life with Bryce Falkirk in America. He loves me and has promised me a part in one of his films. This will be my chance at the big screen. I'd be a fool to let it slip out of my hands. And if I play my cards right he might even ask me to marry him.'

'Have you told him about Georgia?'

Nadia rolled her eyes. 'Are you nuts? Of course I didn't tell him. He thinks Georgia is your child.'

Nina stared at her in alarm. 'How can you even consider the possibility of marrying the man without telling him of your past?'

Nadia gave her sister a cutting look. 'Bryce wouldn't have considered being involved with me at all if I'd told him anything like that. He thinks the sun shines from my "childlike innocent" eyes, and I'm going to make sure he keeps thinking that way, even if I have to lie through my teeth every day to ensure he does.'

'But surely if he really loves you—'

'Look, Nina, I don't want to have the sort of life our mother had, flitting from one bad man to another and shunting kids off into horrible foster homes whenever things got tough. I want to have money and stability and I can't have that with a kid hanging off my hip.'

'But surely you could—'

'No!' Nadia cut her off impatiently. 'You don't get it, do you? I don't want that child; I never did.' She dumped Georgia's changing bag next to the pram, the soft thump as it hit the floor striking a chord of disquiet in Nina's chest. 'You were the one who talked me out of getting rid of the pregnancy, so I think it's only fair you get to look after her now until I can find a private adoption candidate.'

'Private adoption?' Nina instantly stiffened.

Nadia gave her sister a streetwise look. 'There are people out there who will pay big money for a cute little baby. I want to make sure I get the best deal I can. With my connections with Bryce I might even be able to find a Hollywood actor who will want Georgia. Think of the money they would be prepared to pay.'

Nina's eyes flared in shock and her heart began to thump unevenly behind her ribcage. 'How can you do this to your own child?'

'It's none of your business what I do,' Nadia said. 'She's my child, not yours.'

'Let *me* adopt her,' Nina begged. 'I can do it. I'm a blood relative, which would make it so much easier, surely?'

Nadia shook her head. 'No. I'm going to use this opportunity to its fullest extent.' Her eyes glinted with unmistakable avarice. 'It's like a lucky windfall when you think about it. It's my chance to free myself of Andre's child and make a whole heap of money in the process.'

'You're so mercenary.'

'Not mercenary—realistic,' Nadia insisted. 'We might be identical twins but I'm not like you, Nina, and it's high time you accepted it. I want to travel and I want the comfort of wealth and privilege around me. You can keep your long hours in a boring old library—I want a life.'

Nina straightened her shoulders, her chin lifting in pride. 'I enjoy my work.'

'Yeah, well, I enjoy shopping and dining out and partying. And I'm going to do a hell of a lot of it when I get to Bryce's mansion in Los Angeles. I can't wait.'

'I can't believe you're simply going to walk away from your responsibilities. Georgia isn't some sort of toy you can push to one side. She's a baby, for God's sake. Doesn't that mean anything to you at all?'

'No.' Nadia's cold grey eyes clashed with hers. 'It means absolutely nothing to me. I told you—I don't want her.' She scooped up her bag and, rummaging in it, handed her sister a document folder. 'Here is her birth certificate and passport; keep them safe for when it's time to hand her over.' She hoisted her handbag back on to her shoulder and turned for the door.

'Nadia, wait!' Nina cried, glancing at the pram in desperation. 'Aren't you even going to say goodbye to her?'

Nadia opened the door and, with one last determined look, closed it firmly behind her.

Nina knew it would be hopeless running after her to implore her to come back. For most of her twenty-four years she'd been pleading with Nadia to stop and think about her actions, but to no avail. Her wayward and wilful twin had gone from one disaster to another, causing immeasurable hurt in the process and showing little remorse. But this was surely the worst so far.

There was a soft whimper from inside the pram and, moving across the small room, she reached inside to pick up the tiny pink bundle.

'Hey, precious,' she said as she cradled the infant close to her chest, marvelling yet again at the minute perfection of her features. 'Are you hungry, little one?'

The baby began to nuzzle against her and Nina felt a wave of overwhelming love wash through her. She couldn't bear the thought of her niece being handed over to someone else to rear. What if things didn't work out and Georgia's childhood ended up like hers and Nadia's? Nina remembered it all too well— the regular stints in foster care, some of the placements a whole lot less desirable than the neglect she and her twin had received at home. How could she stand by and watch the same thing happen to Georgia?

Nina knew how the legal adoption system worked but this private process made her feel very uneasy. What if someone totally unsuitable offered her sister a huge amount of money? What sort of screening process would the prospective parents go through, if any?

She became aware of the seeping wetness of Georgia's
clothing and, carrying her through to her room, laid her on the
bed and gently undressed her as she'd done countless times before. She got down to the last layer, a tiny yellowed vest that
was frayed at the edges. She peeled it over the tiny child's head,
cooing to her niece as she did so until the soft nonsense of her
words dried up in her throat as she encountered what the vest
had hidden from view. Her eyes widened in shock at the pur-
ple welt of bruises along Georgia's ribcage, bruises that exactly
matched the length and width of her own fingers as if she'd
done the damage herself.

'Oh, Nadia, how could you?' she gulped, fighting back tears
for how she hadn't been able to prevent her niece from suffering what had been commonplace in her own childhood and that
of her twin.

Nina determined then and there that she would do whatever
she could to keep Georgia herself. Surely there was a way to
convince Nadia to give the baby to her permanently.

She had to find one!

Other single mothers coped, so too would she—somehow.

She chewed the ragged edge of one nail as she considered
her options. It wouldn't be easy for her—she could hardly afford childcare on her present salary at the library.

She looked down at the sleeping infant, her chest squeezing painfully at the thought of never seeing her tiny niece again.

No. She would simply not allow her sister to go through with
it.

She would be Georgia's mother and if anyone thought differently, too bad.

No one was going to take her niece away from her.

No one.

Marc Marcello frowned as his secretary informed him via the
office intercom that his father was on the phone from the Villa
Marcello in Sorrento, Italy.

He picked up the receiver and, swivelling in his leather chair, looked out at the expansive view over Sydney Harbour as he pressed the talk button.

'Marc! You have to do something about that woman and do it immediately,' Vito Marcello burst out in rapid-fire Italian.

'I take it you mean Andre's little whore?' Marc answered smoothly.

'She might be a whore but she is also the mother of my only grandchild,' Vito growled.

Marc stiffened in his chair. 'What makes you so certain all of a sudden? Andre refused a paternity test; he said he had always used protection.'

'He might have used protection but I now have reason to believe it failed.'

Marc frowned and turned his chair back to his desk, the sudden thump of his heart in his chest surprising him into a temporary silence.

'I have a letter in front of me with a small photo of the child.' Vito's voice cracked slightly as he continued. 'She looks exactly like Andre at that age. It is Andre's child, I am sure of it.'

Marc pressed his lips together as he fought to get his own raw emotions under some semblance of control. The death of his younger brother had privately devastated him, but for the sake of his terminally ill father he'd carried on the family business without a single hiccup. The Sydney branch of the Marcello merchant bank was booming and he had every intention of maintaining the punishing hours he'd adopted to block out the pain of his brother's death.

'Papa.' His voice was deep and rough around the edges. 'This is all very hard to take in…'

'We have to get that child,' his father insisted. 'She is all we have left of Andre.'

A tremor of unease passed through Marc at the determined edge to his father's tone. 'How do you intend to accomplish this?'

'The usual way,' his father answered with undisguised cynicism. 'If you offer her enough money she will do whatever you ask.'

'How much money are you expecting me to spend on this mission of yours?' Marc asked.

Vito named a figure that sent Marc's broad shoulders to the back of his chair.

'That is a lot of money.'

'I know,' his father agreed. 'But I cannot take the chance that she might not accept your offer. After the response I sent to her previous letter she might avenge my assessment of her character and deny us access to the child.'

Marc inwardly cringed, recalling the content of that letter. His father had emailed him a copy and it had certainly not been complimentary. He could well imagine the Selbourne woman reacting to it out of revenge, particularly if what she said was true—Andre had indeed fathered her child.

He was well aware of Nadia Selbourne's reputation, even though he hadn't met her personally. He'd seen one or two photos, however, which had shown a beautiful woman with thick long blonde hair, eyes that were an unusual smoky grey and the sort of figure that not only turned heads but turned on other parts of the male anatomy at an astonishingly rapid rate as well. His brother had been completely besotted with her until her true character had come out. He could still recall Andre's scathing description of how she had responded when he'd informed her that their short but passionate affair was over. She had hounded him for months, following him and harassing him relentlessly.

But somehow the thought of his dead brother's blood flowing through the tiny veins of her child stirred him both unexpectedly and deeply.

'Marc.' His father's desperate voice cut across his reflections. 'You have to do this. It is a matter of family honour. Andre would have done the same for you if things had been the other way around.'

It was hard for Marc to imagine ever allowing himself to get into the sort of disasters his younger brother had for most of his life, but he didn't think it worthwhile pointing that out now. His father had already suffered enough; he'd lost his beloved son.

It had been no secret in the Marcello family that Andre had always been his father's favourite. His sunny nature and charming boisterous personality had won everyone over virtually from the day he'd been born, leaving Marc with his more serious disposition on the outside.

He frowned as he considered his father's plan. What would it take to convince this woman to hand over the child? Would she take the money and go, or would she insist on something more formal, such as…

His stomach tightened momentarily as he recalled how his brother had told him that Nadia Selbourne was relentless in her search for a rich husband.

But surely his father wouldn't expect him to go *that* far!

So far Marc had managed to ignore the pressure to marry, although he had come very close a few years ago. But it had ended rather badly and he'd actively avoided heavy emotional entanglements since then. Besides, Andre had always made it clear he was going to marry young and father all the Marcello heirs so the family dynasty would be secure. Marc had decided women were not to be trusted where money was involved. And in the Marcello family a *lot* of money was involved.

His heart contracted at the thought of a small dark-haired infant with black-brown eyes—eyes that would one day soon dance with mischief, as her father's had for his too short thirty years of life.

'So will you do it?' Vito pressed. 'Will you do this one thing for me and your late mother?'

Marc pinched the bridge of his Roman nose, his eyes squeezing shut. The mention of his mother always tore at him deeply, the sharp guilt cutting into him until he felt as if he was bleeding. He still remembered that last day, the way she had smiled and waved at him from the other side of the busy street in Rome. She hadn't seen the motor scooter until it had ripped the shopping bags out of her hands, spinning her into the pathway of an oncoming car.

He couldn't help believing that if he had been honest with her about why he was going to be late, maybe she would not have been killed. His father had begged him, and he had honoured him by doing as he'd asked, but the guilt even now was like a deep dark current that dragged at his feet, weighing him down relentlessly.

When his brother had been killed so soon after the death of his mother, Marc hadn't been able to rid himself of the feeling that his father would have grieved a whole lot less if it had been him instead of Andre in that mangled car.

He let out his breath and, releasing his fingers, answered resignedly. 'I will see what I can do…'

'Thank you.' The relief in his father's voice was unmistakable.

Marc knew his father's days were numbered. How much more precious would they be if he could hold his only grandchild in his arms?

'She might refuse to even see me, you know,' Marc warned, thinking again of that vituperative letter his father had sent. 'Have you considered that possibility?'

'Do whatever you have to do to make her see reason,' Vito instructed. 'And I mean anything. This is simply a business arrangement. Women like Nadia Selbourne expect nothing more and nothing less.'

A business arrangement.

What sort of woman was this, Marc thought, who would bargain with the life of a small child?

He put the phone down a few minutes later and turned once more to the sweeping view outside. His dark eyes narrowed against the angle of the sun as he considered what he'd just agreed to do.

He was going to visit the one person he hated more than any other in the world—the woman he believed responsible for his brother's untimely death.

CHAPTER TWO

NINA had not long fed and settled Georgia on Monday morning when the doorbell rang. Giving the small neat room a quick glance, she made her way across the threadbare carpet, wondering what it was that her elderly neighbour wanted now. Ellice Tippen had already borrowed a carton of milk and half a packet of plain biscuits and it wasn't even lunch time.

She opened the door as she plastered a welcoming smile on her face but it instantly faded as her gaze shifted a long way upwards to meet a pair of dark, almost black, eyes.

'Miss Selbourne?'

'I…yes,' she answered, unconsciously putting a hand up to her throat.

The tall figure standing before her was even more arresting in the flesh than the grainy newspaper photo had portrayed. He was taller than average, well over six feet, his shoulders broad and his overall stance nothing short of commanding. The hard angle of his lean clean-shaven jaw hinted at a streak of intractability in his personality, and his eyes held no trace of friendliness. His perfectly tailored business suit superbly highlighted his strong lean body, suggesting he was a man used to a great deal of punishing physical activity.

'I am assuming you know who I am.' His voice was deep and had a hard edge to it as if he wasn't the type to block his punches.

'I…er…yes.'

What else could she say? The weekend paper was still open at his photo on the coffee table behind her. Every time she'd walked past she'd told herself to screw it up and throw it out, but somehow she hadn't. She wasn't entirely sure why.

'I understand you have my brother's child,' he said into the stiff silence.

'I…yes, that's correct.' A vision of Georgia's dark bruises flashed into Nina's mind and her rising panic increased her heart rate to an almost intolerable level. She *had* to keep him away from her niece!

'I would like to see her.'

'I'm afraid she's sleeping just now, so…' She let the sentence trail away, hoping he'd take the hint.

He didn't.

He held her gaze for a lengthy moment and just when she began to close the door he put his foot out to block it.

'Perhaps you did not hear me, Miss Selbourne.' His tone hardened even further as his diamond-hard eyes lasered hers. 'I am here to see my brother's child and I will not be leaving until I do so.'

Nina knew he meant every hard-bitten word and, stepping back from the door, sent him a chilling glance. 'If you wake her I'll be extremely angry.' *Please stay asleep, Georgia,* she silently pleaded as he moved through the doorway, coming to stand right in front of her as the door clicked shut behind him.

He gave her a sweeping up and down look and when his eyes met hers they were full of contempt. 'Andre told me all about you.'

Nina frowned in confusion. She'd never once met her sister's lover. Nadia's affair with him had been brief but explosive, just like all her others.

Surely he didn't think…

'He told me you were trouble, but little did I realise how much,' he continued when she didn't respond.

She stared at him for a moment, wondering if she should disabuse him of his error in thinking she was her sister, but in the end decided to let him go on, to see what his intentions were with regard to Georgia. After all, what harm could it do? All she needed to do was pretend to be Nadia for a few minutes to tell him that she had changed her mind about the letter that had been sent to his father. Once she had convinced him she had no intention of giving up 'her' daughter, hopefully he would go away.

It wasn't as if she hadn't done this type of thing before. So many times in the past Nina had stepped into Nadia's place to take the brunt of whatever punishment their dysfunctional mother had dished out. Surely if she'd been able to hoodwink her own mother, Marc Marcello would be an absolute pushover.

'Your brother's criticism is ironic considering his own behaviour,' she put in crisply.

A menacing glare came into his dark-as-night eyes. 'You dare to malign my dead brother?'

She lifted her chin. 'He was a cheat. While he was fathering Georgia, he was committed elsewhere.'

'He was formally engaged to Daniela Verdacci,' he said bitterly. 'They had been together since they were teenagers. You set your sights on him, no doubt lured by the prospect of his money, but he only ever had eyes for Daniela. Did you really think he would stoop so low as to tie himself permanently to an unprincipled opportunistic little tramp who has slept her way around most of Sydney?'

Nina tensed in anger. She knew her sister had been a little promiscuous at times, but the way Marc Marcello phrased it made it sound as if she had been a call girl instead of the insecure and emotionally unstable person she really was.

'How absolutely typical!' she spat back. 'Why is it men such as yourself and your brother can sow several continents with wild oats but women must not? Get in the real world, Mr Marcello. Women own their sexuality these days and have the same right to express it as you.'

His dark unreadable eyes raked her from head to foot again. 'While we are speaking of rights, the little matter of Andre's child needs to be addressed. As much as I lament and abhor the fact that the child is a Marcello, the fact remains that she is entitled to see her paternal relatives.'

'Surely that decision is up to me?'

'No, I am afraid not, Miss Selbourne.' His voice lowered threateningly. 'Perhaps you do not realise quite who you are dealing with here. The Marcello family will not stand back and watch a street whore raise a blood relative. Unless you do as I say I will do everything in my power to remove her from you so you cannot taint her with your lack of morality.'

Nina's eyes widened in alarm. She was in no doubt of his ability to do as he threatened. There could be few people in Australia who weren't aware of the monumental wealth of the Marcello family. Their influence and control stretched far and wide across the world. With the best legal defence and with a total lack of scruples, she knew it wouldn't be long before Marc Marcello did exactly as he had promised.

Oh, what had Nadia done?

Nina did her best not to appear intimidated, but never had she been more terrified. If he were to find out that she wasn't actually the child's mother, he could remove Georgia right here and now and there would be nothing she could do to stop him.

But he was *not* going to find out. Not if she could help it.

Garnering what courage she could, she stood rigidly before him, her grey eyes issuing a challenge.

'I might appear to be a woman of few morals, but let me assure you I love that child and will not stand back while some overrated playboy sweeps her away. She's a baby and babies need their mothers.'

Marc's gaze swept over her rigid form, noting the tightened line of her full mouth and the stubborn set of her chin. Her startling eyes flashed with venom and, for the first time, he realised just how severely tempted his brother must have been. That pint-sized frame was incredibly alluring, so too the lustrous blonde hair that perfectly offset the creamy quality of her skin. Her figure had snapped back into place rather quickly, he thought, considering she'd not long been delivered of a child. Her air of innocence, however, he knew was the façade of a money-hungry whore who had already demonstrated her intentions by trying to trap his brother with the oldest trick in the book—pregnancy.

'Under normal circumstances I would agree with you,' he said in an even tone. 'Having had the benefit of a wonderful mother, I would be the last person to suggest a child should be raised by anyone else. However, your track record does not inspire the greatest confidence in me that you will be able to support and nurture Andre's child. After all, who was it that sent a missive to my family in Italy stating your intentions to have the child adopted?'

'I…It was a knee-jerk reaction. I was upset and not thinking straight,' she said quickly. 'I have no intention of giving her up. Georgia is mine and no one—and I mean *no one*—is going to remove her from my custody.'

Without warning he stepped towards her, his formidable height casting a dark shadow over her slim form. Nina fought with herself not to shrink away, but it took everything in her to hold herself steady under his threatening presence.

'How remiss of me,' he drawled as he reached inside his suit jacket pocket for his wallet. 'I should have known you would want to twist the screws a bit. How much?'

She looked at him blankly.

One dark aristocratic brow lifted. 'I assume this is what this holding pattern is all about?'

'I have no idea what you're talking about,' she said, her throat suddenly bone-dry.

His mouth twisted into a cynical smile as he fanned open his wallet, 'Come now, Nadia. I am a rich man; I think I can just about afford to pay you off. Name your price.'

Marc was surprised by how much he was enjoying playing with her, seeing her struggle to hold on to her temper, knowing that any minute now she'd cave in to the temptation he was dangling before her beautiful come-to-bed-eyes.

'My real name is Nina and I don't want your stupid money.'

This time both his eyebrows lifted. He paused strategically, wondering what game she was playing now.

'I thought your name was Nadia? I am sure Andre told me it was—or was that a lie too?'

Nina schooled her features into exactly the sort of expression her twin sister was famous for. 'Nina is my real name but I thought Nadia sounded a little more sophisticated. I've since changed my mind.' She inspected her hands in another imitation of her sister before raising her eyes back to his. 'How did you know where to find me?'

'There is only one Miss N Selbourne listed in the phone book in this suburb.'

Since Nadia had moved in with her after the birth of Georgia, her sister's erratic approach to paying bills meant that Nina had left the telephone in her name alone, which had obviously made it even easier for Marc to assume she was her twin.

She allowed one tiny inaudible breath of relief to escape the tight frame of her lips.

So far so good.

'Well, then…*Nina*.' He drew her name out suggestively. 'If you are not after money, what do you want?'

'Nothing.'

The cynical smile was back. 'It has been my experience that women like you are always after money even when they insist to the contrary.'

'Your experience must be terribly limited, for I can assure you I have no need of your money.'

'Not mine, perhaps, but you must be aware that my dead brother has left a considerable estate. You have given birth to his child, which means she has a legal right to claim some, if not all, of that estate when she comes of age.'

Nina swallowed. This was getting more and more complicated by the minute.

'I'm not interested in Andre's estate.'

'You expect me to believe that?' he growled. 'Behind those eyes of yours I can see the dollar signs already rolling in anticipation.' His dark gaze left hers to sweep the room before coming back to glare down at her. 'Look at this place! It reeks of poverty and neglect. Do you think I will allow my niece to live in such a hovel?'

Nina felt pride straighten her spine. 'It's all I can afford at present.'

He gave a harsh laugh. 'At present is right. No doubt you have already got some other poor unsuspecting man in your sights for your next free ride.' He gave her a look of undiluted disgust and continued. 'You must be offering something pretty special underneath that "butter would not melt in your mouth" pose for anyone to take you on with another man's baby in tow.'

Nina had never considered herself a volatile person; Nadia had been the firebrand, her unpredictable mood swings causing many an unpleasant scene. But somehow, hearing Marc's disdain, even though it was directed at her twin, bit her deeply and on her sister's behalf she fought back.

'Are you offering to take up where Andre left off?' she asked in a tone dripping with sultry provocation.

His dark eyes glittered with hatred so intense it secretly unnerved her.

'I can see how you want to play this,' he said after another nerve-tightening pause.

'On the contrary, I want nothing other than for you to leave my home immediately. You're not the least bit interested in my n...er...daughter.' She took a quick breath to disguise her vocal stumble. 'If you don't leave then I will have no other choice than to call the police and have you thrown out.'

Black eyes clashed with grey for endless seconds but finally Nina was the first to lower her gaze.

'Please leave, Mr Marcello. I have nothing else I wish to say to you.'

'I want to see my niece.' His adamant tone brought her eyes back to his. 'I want to see the child my brother fathered.'

Nina pressed her lips together as she saw the struggle he made to keep his emotions under control. She heard it in his voice and saw it in his rigid stance as he faced her, his dark eyes shining with sudden moisture.

She hadn't expected him to have such depth of human feeling and it shamed her to realise how seriously she'd misjudged him. After all, she reminded herself, he had not long buried his only sibling under tragic circumstances. Even with all Nadia's distressing foibles, she knew that in the same situation she would be little less than devastated.

'I'm sorry.' Her voice came out unevenly.

His mouth twisted. 'Are you?'

She didn't answer but moved past him to the pram under the single window. She was conscious of his tall frame just behind her as she peeled back the covers so he could see Georgia's face.

She felt him standing close beside her, his arm brushing hers as he looked down at his brother's child for a long time without speaking. The silence was so intense she could hear the sound of his breathing, his chest moving in and out with the effort of controlling his reaction to seeing his niece for the first time.

'Can I hold her?'

Nina felt as if her heart had done a complete somersault in her chest at his simple request. What if he held her the wrong way and she cried?

'Um…I don't think—'

'Please.' His raw tone brought her eyes back to his. 'I would like to hold my brother's child. She is all that I have left of him.'

Nina released an uneven breath and carefully lifted the sleeping baby from amongst the covers, cradling her gently before turning and handing her to him.

She watched as a thousand emotions flashed over his handsome features as he brought the tiny bundle close to his broad chest, his dark gaze thoughtful as he looked down at the perfection of Georgia's peaceful face.

'She is…beautiful.' His tone was distinctly husky.

Nina had trouble keeping the emotion out of her own voice. 'Yes, she is.'

His eyes met hers briefly. 'What did you call her?'

She lowered her gaze a fraction. 'Georgia.'

'Georgia,' he repeated as if tasting it. 'It suits her.'

She chanced a look at him and was surprised to see how at ease he was holding the infant, one of his large hands cradling her securely while the other explored her miniature features as if in wonder.

'Does she have a middle name?' he asked into the heavy silence.

'Grace,' she answered, wondering if she should tell him it was her own middle name, but at the last minute deciding against it. She'd been so touched when Nadia had told her of her choice of names, and for a while had hoped her sister was going to finally settle down and face her responsibilities. But within a few short weeks of Georgia's birth she had gone back to late-night partying and drinking, leaving the baby with Nina so often that Georgia had begun to cry whenever Nadia had made any approach at all, as if sensing her total inadequacy as a carer.

Nina was increasingly aware of the silence in the room as Marc Marcello held his niece, his dark gaze fixed on the child's face.

She said the first thing that came into her head. 'I think she looks like Andre, don't you?'

Marc swung his gaze to where she was standing, his hard

expression instantly clouding. She thought he was going to agree with her but instead he turned back to the child in his arms and asked, looking down at her, 'Did he ever see her?'

'No.'

She'd been furious when Nadia had told her that Andre hadn't wanted to see his baby, and couldn't help wondering if that was the reason her sister hadn't bonded with the child in the first place. The whole way through the pregnancy Nadia had had all her hopes pinned on Andre falling in love with his child once he saw her, thus ensuring a secure future for Nadia as his wife. When he had flatly refused to take a paternity test to establish whether or not the baby was his, Nadia had gone into a deep depression, closely followed by a spate of reckless partying.

'No,' she repeated, her tone holding a distinct note of bitterness. 'I expect he was too busy preparing for his wedding.'

Marc didn't answer but Nina could see the sudden tightening of his jaw as if her words had annoyed him.

She watched as he laid the baby down once more, his touch sure but gentle as he tucked the light bunny rug back into place.

When he turned to face her she found it difficult to hold his piercing gaze as she thought of how she was deceiving him. It suddenly occurred to her what a dangerous game she was playing. Wasn't there some sort of law against impersonating another person? Marc Marcello was nobody's fool and if he were to ever find out how he'd been duped there would be hell to pay, she was sure.

'Miss Selbourne.' His deep voice brought her troubled gaze back to his.

'Y-yes?' She moistened her lips, somehow sensing he was going to state his intentions, all her instincts telling her she wasn't going to like them one little bit.

'I want to see my niece on a regular basis and, while I understand your aversion to such an arrangement, I think you know I will pursue this legally if you refuse.'

'I'm her mother,' she bit out. 'No court in Australia would remove her from my custody.'

'You think not?' His lip curled. 'What if I told them about your little affair with a certain prominent politician just a few weeks after giving birth to my brother's child?'

What affair? Nina thought in panic. What politician? What the hell had Nadia been up to?

He must have seen the flicker of alarm cross her features as he added in a cool deliberate tone, 'You see, Miss Selbourne, I have all the dirt on you and I intend to use it in order to bring about what I want. I have heard how you tried to extort money from the poor fool when he called a halt to the relationship. You have been lucky that little affair did not get the press's attention, but one word from me and, well…' He paused for effect. 'You know the rest.'

She sucked in a ragged breath, even her fingertips growing icy cold with dread as it spread through her body like the flow of mercury in her veins.

'What exactly do you want?' Her words came out like hard pellets.

Marc waited for a few moments before he answered. Until he had seen Andre's child—and one look told him she was indeed his—he had not really thought much further than waving a truckload of money under the mother's nose and walking away with the baby as his father had planned. But somehow seeing Nina with the baby, the way she looked at Georgia so lovingly and cradled her so gently, he wasn't convinced that he would be acting in the best interests of his niece by removing her from her mother, unless he was absolutely sure she was not up to the task of caring for her. If indeed he could, considering that ill-judged letter of his father's, and its vicious rejection of the baby. The woman had a powerful weapon there, if she chose to use it.

Which left him with only one other course of action.

His obsidian gaze held hers determinedly. 'I want to claim my brother's child as my own.'

'You can't do that! She doesn't belong to you! She belongs t-to…t-to me.'

'I can, you know.'

'How?'

She shouldn't have asked, Nina thought later. She just should never have asked.

His dark eyes locked with hers and a persistent tickling feather of fear began to tease its way up the entire length of her spine.

'I want that baby and I will do anything to have her, even if it means I have to tie myself to you to do so.'

She blinked at him, wondering if she'd misinterpreted his chilling statement. 'Tie yourself? What do you mean *tie* yourself?'

His mouth twisted into a smile that didn't quite reach his dark-as-sin eyes. 'My brother refused to marry you, but I have no such scruples. You will be my wife within a fortnight or I will make sure you never see your daughter again.' He kept his features still, knowing his bluff was convincing. But would it work?

It took Nina a moment or two to find her voice, her head pounding with a combination of shock and outrage.

'Do you seriously think I will be coerced in such a way?' she finally spat indignantly.

'I am more or less counting on it. Andre told me your main goal in life was to land a rich husband, so here I am, ready to step into the role.'

She opened her mouth to speak again but her throat closed over at the steely determination in his dark gaze as it clashed with hers.

She considered coming clean, telling him she was really Nadia's twin, hoping he would understand her need to protect her niece, but his air of icy hauteur changed her mind at the last minute. She'd be damned if she would give up her niece without a furious fight, even if it cost her everything she had, including her freedom.

She flashed him a look of pure loathing at the way he'd cleverly herded her into a corner from which she could increasingly see there might be little chance of escape. She saw the glint of anticipated victory in his dark gaze and her blood ebbed and flowed through her veins in a tide of anger and growing fear.

'I suppose it's to be expected a spoilt playboy like you would assume he can always get whatever he wants,' she said.

'I will, of course, pay you generously,' he said, his dark eyes watching her steadily. 'How much do you want?'

Nina was very conscious that in her place Nadia would have asked for some outrageous sum, but something stopped her from taking the charade that far. The ice she'd inadvertently skated on to was suddenly very thin in places, but taking money in what was little more than a bribe was surely going to lead to more trouble than she could cope with at present.

Besides, little Georgia was lying asleep less than a metre away from him, her tiny body badly bruised. She'd been lucky this time but if he took even one look beneath that vest…

Forcing her chin upwards, she tilted her head at him, her arms folded in front of her chest, and informed him with unintentional irony, 'If you think you can bribe me then you've got the wrong person.'

His eyes flicked to her where her breasts were pushed up by her folded arms, taking his time before returning to her face.

Nina stood silently fuming under his mocking appraisal, wondering how in the world her sister's behaviour had brought her to this. She knew her anger should be directed at Nadia and not the man before her, but everything about him goaded her beyond bearing.

'I told you before, I don't want your money. I'd feel tainted by taking anything from you.'

'Nice try, Miss Selbourne,' he drawled back. 'I can see what you are doing. You are pretending to be nothing like the avaricious young woman who seduced my brother, but I can see through your little act. Do not think that you can deceive me so easily; I have made up my mind, and you will do as I say, whether you accept payment from me or not.'

Nina did her best to hide how his statement affected her while her mind raced on, wondering how in the world she was going to get out of this farcical situation. God, she was going to kill Nadia for this! Surely she couldn't be forced to marry the man just to keep her niece? But what else was she to do? Nadia was an unfit mother and—like her—Marc apparently had enough evidence to prove it.

'I want some time to think about this.' She was a little unnerved by how like Nadia she sounded, but carried on regardless. 'I like to look at all the angles on things before I commit myself.'

'I am not here to negotiate, Miss Selbourne,' he said intractably. 'I am here to step into the role of Georgia's father and I want to do it as soon as possible.'

She looked up at him in growing alarm. There was an intransigent edge to his tone that suggested he was well used to getting his own way and would go to any lengths at his disposal to do so.

Tell him the truth, she mentally chanted. *Tell him who you really are.* But the words were stuck somewhere in the middle of her chest where her heart was already squeezing at the thought of never seeing Georgia again.

She tried to think rationally and clearly but it was hard with him standing there watching every tiny flicker of emotion on her face.

What if she went along with his demands for now? He'd said two weeks. Surely she'd be able to wriggle out of it by then. Hopefully Nadia would be in contact soon and she'd be able to sort something out. She *had* to sort something out. She couldn't possibly marry a perfect stranger!

Marc took her continued silence as acquiescence. 'I will have the necessary papers drawn up immediately.'

'But…' She stopped, her heart giving another funny skip in her chest. Oh, God! What had she done? Surely he wasn't serious?

She tried again. 'H-how soon do you want me to...' She found it hard to finish the sentence as his hard eyes cut to hers with a look of total disdain.

'Perhaps I should make something very clear at this point. I do not want *you*, Miss Selbourne. This will not be a proper marriage in the true sense of the word.'

'Not legal, do you mean?' She frowned, trying to make sense of his meaning.

'It will be legal, I would not settle for less, but it will be a paper marriage only.'

'A paper marriage?' Her finely arched brows met above her eyes.

'We will not be consummating the relationship,' he stated implacably.

Nina knew she should be feeling overwhelming relief at his curt statement but for some inexplicable reason she felt annoyed instead. She knew she wasn't looking as glamorous right now as Nadia customarily did, but her figure was good and her features classically appealing. It didn't sit that well with her to have him dismiss her desirability so readily, as if she held no physical appeal at all.

'You expect me to trust you on that?' she asked with just the right amount of cynicism in her tone.

He lifted a long-fingered tanned hand and made a sign of a cross over his chest as his eyes pinned hers.

'Cross my heart and hope to die.'

Something about his air of supreme confidence tempted Nina into giving him the sort of seductive look she'd seen her sister casting men's way for years. She placed her hand on her hip as she tilted her pelvis provocatively, the corners of her mouth tipping upwards in a taunting little salacious smile as she drawled breathily, 'Then I would say you're as good as a dead man, Mr Marcello.'

CHAPTER THREE

MARC gave an inward smile at her overblown confidence. She was just as Andre had described, all pouting little girl one minute, raging sex siren the next. It was a heady combination, he had to admit, but while Andre hadn't been able to contain his desire for her, temporary as it had been, Marc felt confident he was in no danger of being tested beyond his control. Nina Selbourne was the total opposite of what he most wanted in a partner.

He loathed shallow money-hungry women who had nothing better to do than preen themselves in the hope of attracting a rich husband. He'd been surrounded by them for most of his life, with the exception of his French-born mother, who had had both style and grace without affectation.

No, Miss Nina/Nadia Selbourne was fooling herself if she thought he would fall for her physical charms.

'I am not like my brother, Miss Selbourne,' he informed her coldly. 'My tastes are a little more upmarket.'

Nina wished she could slap that imperious smirk off his handsome face but knew there would probably be distasteful consequences if she did. She clenched her hands into fists and glared back at him.

'I could make you eat those words and we both know it. I saw the way you ran your eyes all over me the moment I opened the door.'

'I admit I was a little intrigued as to what made my brother act so incautiously.' His lazy look took in her heaving chest and feisty gaze. 'But I can assure you I have no appetite for vacuous women such as yourself.'

Nina schooled her features back under control with difficulty. 'I take it this marriage arrangement you're proposing leaves you free to liaise with whomever you want whenever you want?'

'I will do my best to be discreet if the need should arise.'

'What about me?' she asked. 'Am I allowed to indulge myself similarly?'

He didn't answer immediately but she could almost hear the cogs of his brain ticking over as he considered her question.

'Well?' she prodded with an arch look.

'No.'

'No?'

He shook his head in slow motion, 'Absolutely not.'

'You can't possibly be serious.' She snapped her brows together again.

'Deadly serious,' he said and folded his arms across the broad expanse of his chest.

'You surely don't expect me to agree to such a double standard?' she asked. 'What am I supposed to get out of this arrangement?'

'You get to keep your child, with a rich husband thrown in as a bonus.'

She let out her breath in a whoosh of feminist outrage. 'I thought men like you died along with the dinosaurs. Seems I was wrong. So, how are things on Planet Chauvinism these days?'

'I am not by nature a chauvinist but I am sure it will do you good to be celibate for a while to concentrate on your responsibilities as a mother.'

Ironic laughter bubbled to her lips before she could stop it. Unlike her sister, who had lost her virginity at the age of fourteen, Nina was technically still a virgin. Technically because she firmly believed every modern woman had the right to explore her own body and find out how things worked, although she still wondered what all the fuss was about. The earth hadn't exactly moved and she'd more or less given up on herself, deciding she was one of those women with unusually low sex-drives. But on principle she wasn't going to let him have things all his way. He already thought her the biggest tart outside of the red-light district and a perverse little part of her was enjoying every dangerous minute of encouraging him to maintain that view.

'You find the prospect of being responsible amusing?' His tone dripped with contempt.

She coiled a strand of her long hair around one finger, hoping he wouldn't notice her chewed nail as she affected another seductive pose.

'You're a laugh a minute, Mr Marcello,' she said. 'All this talk of being celibate is hilarious. I haven't been celibate for ten years and I'm not about to start for you or anyone.'

Anger briefly flashed across his features as he looked down at her. Nina saw his hands tighten into fists as if he didn't trust himself not to reach out and touch her.

A flicker of sensation unexpectedly erupted between her thighs at the mere thought of any part of his tall hard body touching her. She began to imagine what that firm disapproving mouth would feel like crushed to hers, his tongue searching arrogantly to duel with hers. She felt her breasts start to tingle and, almost without realising she was doing it, her tongue came out just a fraction to sweep over the surface of her lips.

Marc felt the sharp tug of sudden errant desire hit him in the belly like a closed fist punch. He struggled to control it, annoyed with himself for being tempted when he'd been so assured that he would be able to resist her, but something about her struck at him deeply. She positively oozed with sexual confidence, the smoky grey of her eyes and full-lipped mouth making his skin lift in anticipation of feeling her touch.

He decided to strike a deal with her even though he had cause to wonder if he was shooting himself in the foot in the process.

'Since you seem unwilling to agree to my terms, I am willing to make a small compromise,' he announced. 'For the period of one month following our marriage we will both remain celibate; how about that?'

She pursed her lips as if considering it. 'One month? Hmm…I think I could just about manage that.'

His jaw tightened and she gave him another sexy smile. 'But no longer or I'll go out of my mind. But then, from what I hear of you—' she ran her eyes over him from head to foot as if undressing him thread by thread '—maybe you will too.'

'I think I will manage to contain myself,' he responded coolly.

'I take it you don't have a current mistress?' She sent him a lash-fluttering glance.

'I am not currently close to anyone.'

Nina couldn't help wondering how good he might be when he was *close*. He was the whole knee-trembling spine-loosening package, even though it irked her to admit it. He was handsome beyond belief, his dark mesmerizing eyes promising explosive passion from within their glittering depths. His mouth was currently stretched into a hardened line of derision but she was in no doubt of its power to persuade if he allowed himself a moment of weakness and brought his head down to hers.

The pram near the window suddenly gave a squeak of protest as Georgia shifted in her sleep.

Marc swung his gaze to the pram before turning back to face Nina, his voice low and deep with concern. 'Is she all right?'

Sending him a now-see-what-you've-done look, Nina went over to soothe her. The mewing cries stopped as soon as her hand stroked Georgia's tiny legs, the gentle rhythmic movements sending the infant back to sleep within a couple of minutes.

Nina was intensely aware of the watchful gaze of Marc Marcello a short distance away. She could almost sense his cool assessment of her, no doubt weighing up her skills as a mother.

Once she was sure the baby was soundly asleep she turned and faced him, her grey eyes meeting his with as much equanimity as she could.

'You said earlier you intended to marry within two weeks. Why the hurry?'

'My father is terminally ill. He wishes to see his only grandchild before he dies. There is not much time.'

'A fortnight isn't very long.' She gave her bottom lip a surreptitious nibble.

'I will see to all the details. You do not have to do anything but turn up at the registry office.'

Nina knew it was pathetic of her to be feeling disappointed, but if by some quirk of fate she had to go through with this, her lifelong dream of a beautiful white wedding in a city cathedral was going to have to be shelved indefinitely.

'But what about a dress?' she asked, trying not to think of Marc Marcello's motives for marrying her.

'I have no real interest in what sort of outfit you wear,' he said. 'However, I do think it would be highly inappropriate of you to wear white.' His eyes flicked to the pram and back again. 'Don't you?'

She held his gaze for as long as she dared. 'I happen to like wearing white. It suits my colouring.'

Marc was certain she'd still look stunning even if she was covered from head to foot in a nun's habit. Her come-to-bed eyes had tugged far too many men into their seductive orbit and he had to make sure he didn't join their number.

'Wear what you like; the ceremony will be over within minutes anyway. I will make an appointment with my lawyer to draw up the necessary paperwork.' He made a move towards the door, slanting a warning look her way. 'I should remind you at this point that if you wish to pull out of the deal I will have no choice but to activate proceedings to remove Georgia permanently from your custody. And do not think I cannot do it, for I assure you I can and will if I need to.'

Nina wished she could throw his threat back at him but the thought of losing her niece was just too wrenching. She knew he only had to see those fading but still present bruises on Georgia's tiny chest for the fight to be over right here and now.

She only hoped that maybe in time Marc would see how much she too loved the baby and wanted the best for her. But what would he do if or when he found out the truth?

'I won't pull out of the deal,' she said, wishing her voice hadn't sounded quite so hollow.

'No, I imagine not.' His eyes held hers with a caution reflected in their glittering depths 'I will, of course, be providing you with an allowance for the duration of our marriage.'

Nina instantly stiffened, but for some reason couldn't find her voice.

'What will you do with all that money to spend, I wonder?' he mused insultingly.

She gave him one of her sister's casual shrugs. 'Shop and shop and shop, probably.'

Marc's lip curled distastefully. 'You are a complete and utter sybarite. Have you ever done a decent day's work in your life?'

'Work?' She wrinkled her nose in repugnance. 'Why work when you can have fun instead?'

'I must be out of my mind,' he muttered under his breath. 'You sicken me. I can hardly believe you lured my brother away from Daniela. She postponed the wedding because of you. If you hadn't come along when you did, Andre—'

'How typical to blame the woman in the middle,' she shot back furiously on her sister's behalf. 'He didn't have to sleep with me; he could always have said no.'

'You hounded him for months,' he tossed back. 'He told me how determined you were, how it became impossible to keep you at arm's length.'

'I think I can safely say he enjoyed it while it lasted. And I bet you would too. I can guarantee it.'

'Sorry to disappoint you, but that will not be happening. You know the score and if you put one foot out of place I will use all the weapons at my disposal.'

Nina could well believe it. He quite possibly had cards up his sleeve that could prove to be a little too tactical for her liking. She had two weeks to think of a way out and she was going to do her best to find one, for it was becoming increasingly clear she was seriously outmatched in her opponent.

'Will any of your relatives be attending the ceremony?' she asked in an effort to hide her disquiet.

'No, my father is unable to travel and my mother is…' He hesitated slightly before continuing. 'She died a couple of years ago.'

Nina couldn't help feeling a wave of sympathy for his father, who had been dealt a double blow of grief in losing his son so close to the death of his wife. She imagined Marc was dealing with overwhelming grief too and it made her anger towards his treatment of her soften around the edges.

'It must be a very difficult time for you all,' she said gently.

Marc threw her a look of disgust. 'How dare you offer sympathy when if it had not been for you, my brother would still be alive?'

Nina stared at him in shock. This was getting even worse than a nightmare. What did he mean?

'That's a heavy accusation,' she managed to get out. 'Exactly what evidence do you have to substantiate it?'

'You were the last person to see Andre before he went to pick up Daniela from the airport.'

Nina hadn't known that little detail and wondered why her sister hadn't mentioned it.

'So?' She made her voice sound as unconcerned as possible even though her stomach was rolling in consternation.

'Daniela was understandably upset at what had gone on

whilst she had been in Milan visiting her family the first time,'
he said. 'She was threatening to call off the wedding altogether
but Andre was adamant that his involvement with you had
ceased. She knew about the baby and it caused a great deal of
trouble between them, as she was concerned about him having further contact with you. She lived long enough after the
accident to tell me that Andre had been on edge when he arrived to pick her up, as you had visited him the night before
making your usual outrageous demands. He had not slept well
after you left and his concentration was all over the place. A
truck ran a red light and he did not have the necessary reaction
time to avoid the collision.'

'And you think that's my fault?' Nina asked tightly. 'I wasn't
driving the truck!'

'You might as well have been, as far as I am concerned.
Andre was deeply ashamed of himself for getting involved
with you. It almost destroyed his relationship with Daniela.'

'He should have thought about the consequences before he
gave me the come-on,' she threw back.

'Have you not got that the wrong way around?' he asked
with a flash of black eyes. 'It was not Andre who was lying
naked in the hotel bed that first night—it was you.'

Nina did her best to hide her shock at his statement. There
was so much she didn't know and the further she became em-
broiled in this farce the harder it was to maintain her cover.
Nadia had told her virtually nothing, which meant she now had
to lie her way through this emotional minefield.

Lie after lie after lie.

She'd read somewhere that if a person were to tell one lie
they then had to go on and tell thousands to keep that single
one in place. Now she could well believe it.

'So?' She tried the casual tone again. 'He could have said no.'

'There are very few men who could say no when such temptation is dangled in front of them,' he said, raking his gaze over
her once more.

Nina tilted her head at him provocatively. 'So you admit to being a little tempted yourself?'

His hand left the doorknob as he strode back across the room to stand in front of her, his expression so full of hatred she had to force herself not to step backwards to escape the heat of it coming off him in scorching waves.

His eyes burned down into hers forcefully, the inky depths glittering as if he was only just managing to keep his temper under control.

'You might have the body of a goddess and the face of an angel but I would not touch you even if you held the key to life itself,' he ground out heavily.

Injured feminine pride made Nina hitch up her chin another fraction, her eyes issuing him a challenge she knew deep inside she should not be issuing but she just couldn't help it. How dare he dismiss her so confidently?

'Want to lay a bet on that, big boy? Put your money where your mouth is—so to speak.'

The line of his mouth grew even tighter until his lips appeared almost white. Nina could tell she had taken things a little too far but it was too late to back out now.

'All right.' He finally released his breath. 'I will lay a bet on it. If I touch you other than in the most casual way during our marriage, you win the bet. I will double your allowance on the spot.'

She suddenly realised that Nadia would have asked how much he intended giving her by now but it simply hadn't occurred to Nina to do so.

'Um…how much are you intending to pay me?'

'Much more than you are worth, I can assure you.'

Her eyes burned with seething hatred at his denigration, everything inside her quaking with anger until she could barely stand still. She felt it rumbling in her stomach, flash-flooding her veins as it was carried to every single cell of her body.

'That remains to be seen,' she said in Nadia's confident

flirty tone even though her teeth were being ground to powder behind her seductive smile.

His midnight eyes gleamed with confidence as he looked down at her, the small smile that was playing on his lips a combination of both mockery and challenge.

'Go ahead, Miss Selbourne, go ahead and make me pay.'

She opened her mouth to respond but before she could get the words out the door opened under his hand and he stepped through and closed it behind him with an ominous click of the lock as it fell back into place.

She stared at the door for a moment or two, her stomach in tight knots of panic, her head throbbing with tension and her legs trembling at the thought of what she'd just done.

She turned and leaned heavily on the arm of the old sofa, her frazzled brain trying to find a satisfactory way out of her predicament.

If she told him who she really was he would have even more reason to claim Georgia, for she could hardly provide for her the way he obviously could and, with Nadia already abandoning her daughter, what hope would there be of fighting back?

But marrying him?

Her heart gave another heavy thump of panic at the thought of being formally tied to him in marriage, all the time having to keep her true identity a secret. But unless Nadia reappeared and claimed her daughter, Nina knew she was going to have to continue with the charade for as long as necessary. What other choice was there? Georgia needed her. She couldn't let her down.

Two weeks…that was all she had and it wasn't anywhere near long enough.

She gave a tiny shiver as she thought of him towering over her the way he had, his eyes aflame with dislike. He was ruthlessness and power personified; he was used to simply paying for any obstacles in his path to be removed and she would be the first to be crushed beneath his well-heeled foot.

She gave a little jump when the telephone rang on the small table beside her and, reaching out a still shaking hand, picked up the receiver and held it to her ear.

'Nina?' Nadia's voice rang out airily. 'I thought I'd call you en route. I'm in Singapore for a couple of hours while the plane refuels.'

'Do you have any idea of what you've done?' Nina choked, clutching at the receiver with both hands.

'I know you don't approve of me leaving Georgia,' Nadia said. 'But quite frankly I don't care. I want—'

'Will you shut up and listen to me?' Nina bit out. 'How could you do that to your own daughter? Not only did you abandon her but you hurt her!'

'Look.' Nadia's tone hardened. 'She was crying for ages while you were out. It drove me nuts.'

Nina's stomach churned at the thought of the abuse happening under her very own roof.

'She's a defenceless child. You were one once; don't you remember what it feels like to be so vulnerable?'

'I don't remember a thing, so drop it, OK?'

Nina sighed with frustration. Her twin was an expert at burying her head when things got tough. There was nothing she could say or do to change the habits of a lifetime. Her sister was damaged and all she could do now was accept it and do what she could to protect Georgia from repeating the pattern in her own life.

'Any news from Andre's people?' Nadia asked as casually as if asking what the afternoon's weather had been like in her absence.

'He came here,' Nina said through clenched teeth.

'Who?'

'You damn well know who!' She felt close to screaming. 'Marc in-your-face Marcello.'

'I thought he might.'

'How can you be so casual about this?' Nina cried. 'He thinks I'm *you,* for God's sake!'

Nadia hooted with laughter. 'Does he really? How amusing.'

'Well, guess what—I'm not laughing,' Nina ground out. 'And you'd better get back here as soon as you can and sort it out.'

'I'm not coming back,' Nadia said determinedly. 'Bryce is expecting me in LA tomorrow. Why don't you just tell him who you are and be done with it?'

Nina whooshed out a breath. 'Because he wants Georgia, that's why.'

'Does he now?' Nadia's sugar-sweet voice grated along Nina's shredded nerves. 'So the photograph did the trick then.'

'What do you mean?'

Nina heard the sound of her sister's long artificial nails tapping a nearby surface as if she was mentally planning something.

'He'll have to pay, of course, but it's where she belongs anyway. Think of how rich she'll be when she comes of age, an entire family of billionaire merchant bankers to call on for a loan or two.'

'I can't believe you can be so unfeeling about this,' Nina said reproachfully. 'Do you know what he means to do?'

'What?' Nadia's tone sounded bored.

'He's forcing me—I mean you—to marry him, which is really me because you've flown the coop and he doesn't realise it, and I'm up to my neck in lies and I don't know if I can face it because I have no idea how to handle men like Marc Marcello and I have work commitments and no childcare and—'

'Whoa!' Nadia interjected. 'Slow down; you lost me at the marriage bit. What do you mean he wants to marry you?'

'Not me—*you!*' Nina shrilled. 'He thinks he's forcing *you* into a paper marriage.'

'A paper marriage?'

'He wants to adopt Georgia and is prepared to marry me— I mean *you*—to do it.'

'And you agreed?' Nadia sounded surprised.

'He didn't really leave me with much choice,' Nina answered resentfully. 'He threatened to expose you as an incompetent mother and you gave him all the evidence he needed by hurting Georgia the way you did. It was just pure luck that he didn't notice—'

'What's he paying you?' Nadia asked.

Nina gritted her teeth at her sister's total lack of remorse. How could Nadia be more concerned about money than her own baby?

'Even if I have to starve I am not taking his money,' she bit out. 'He thinks he can buy me but no way is some overindulged playboy going to—'

'Tell him you've changed your mind,' Nadia said, interrupting her again. 'Tell him you want ten million.'

'Ten million?' Nina shrieked. 'I will do no such—'

'Then you're a fool,' Nadia said. 'He's a billionaire, Nina. You can name your price. He'll pay it.'

'No, absolutely not. This marriage thing is bad enough.' She let out a ragged breath and added, 'Besides, I feel sick at the thought of what he's going to do when he finds out he's got the wrong person.'

'Don't tell him.'

'What?' Nina squeaked. 'You expect me to go through with it?'

'You want Georgia, don't you?' Nadia said. 'Here's your chance to keep her with a whole trailer load of money thrown in. In fact, if you play your cards right we could both really scoop up big time on this.'

Nina didn't care too much for her twin's mercenary tone. 'What do you mean?'

Nadia gave a soft little chuckle that sent a river of unease up her spine. 'You are about to marry a billionaire. You will have access to cash, lots and lots of cash. I've been doing some checking up on Bryce and he's not quite in the same league as your Marc. But we can make up for that with some clever accounting on your part once you are married.'

Nina cleared the blockage in her tight throat. 'Nadia, I can't marry Marc Marcello! It wouldn't be legal!'

'Who's going to know?' Nadia asked airily. 'As far as I recall, I didn't tell Andre I had a twin, so his brother is unlikely to ever find out unless you tell him or he sees us together, which is hardly likely as I'm going to be on the other side of the globe. No, the more I think about this the better it sounds. We both stand to benefit. You get to keep Georgia and I get compensated by a regular income provided by your very rich husband.'

Nina felt her stomach drop in panic. 'Nadia, please don't do this to me. I can't marry a man who hates the very air I breathe!'

'He doesn't hate you, he hates me,' Nadia pointed out. 'Anyway, once he gets to know you he might even fancy you, or at least he might if you'd whack on a bit of make-up and something other than a shapeless tracksuit from time to time.'

'I can't afford the sort of scraps of fabric you usually pipe yourself into,' Nina said sourly.

'Come on, Nina. Think about it. This is a chance in a lifetime. You've always wanted to get married and have kids. What are you complaining about?'

'I would have liked to choose the groom for myself, that's what I'm complaining about!' Nina shot back. 'And I wanted a church wedding, not some hole and corner affair at the local registry office.'

'You're such a hopeless romantic. Do you think a marriage has any more hope of survival if it's performed in a church? Come on—get in the real world, Nina. Marrying a billionaire should more than make up for the absence of a dress and veil and the blessing of a priest.'

'Yeah, well, somehow it just doesn't,' she answered. 'I wanted more out of life than a rich husband.'

'You could spend your whole life looking for love like our mother did and, just like her, never find it,' Nadia said. 'If I were you I'd grasp at this with both hands and make the most of it.'

'But I'm not you, am I?' Nina reminded her coolly.

'No.' A hint of amusement entered Nadia's voice again. 'But Marc Marcello doesn't know that, does he?'

CHAPTER FOUR

NINA called in sick at the library the next day in order to sort out childcare arrangements but her efforts were not encouraging. As she didn't have a car, she was limited to using a private centre whose fees were extortionate. She had no choice but to make the booking, hoping that her niece would cope with the change without too much fuss.

The next two days passed without any further contact from Marc. At times Nina wondered if she'd imagined the whole thing, so unreal it seemed, but on the third day a letter arrived, the first page of the thick document informing her that the marriage ceremony would be on July the fifteenth.

She felt her spine buckle in trepidation. It seemed there was no way out. She would have to marry Marc in order to keep Georgia. She would have to continue to deceive him, even though in doing so she was going to be fuelling his hatred even more.

The thought of pretending to be her sister for months, maybe even years on end, terrified her but she couldn't see any alternative. It was incredible to think that a few simple words stood between her and her freedom. If she told him: 'I am not Georgia's mother', the marriage would be called off.

Five words and she would be free.

Five simple words that would grant her instant freedom, but take away her niece—permanently.

As she had more or less expected, there had been no further

contact from Nadia. Nina had tried her mobile repeatedly, but each time the message service informed her the phone was out of service, and the numerous text messages she'd sent went unanswered. As her sister hadn't given her a forwarding address it made it even more impossible for Nina to escape the tight net that was surrounding her minute by minute.

She tossed the letter from Marc aside to respond to Georgia's cries for attention, doing her best to keep her mind away from the thought of being married to a man who hated her so much.

As she came back out to the small sitting room with Georgia tucked close to her, the phone rang and she reached to answer it.

'Nina.' Marc's deep voice sounded in her ear. 'It's Marc.'

'Marc who?' She was back in Nadia's personality as if by simply hearing his smooth as melted chocolate voice an internal switch had flicked back on inside her.

She heard his indrawn breath and mentally congratulated herself for winning this small battle even though she knew he was more than likely to win the war in the end.

'I am quite sure with the reputation you have worked on so assiduously you have doubled up on some names by now,' he drawled insolently.

'Wouldn't you like to know,' she threw back.

'Did you get my letter?'

'Let me see…' She rustled the small collection of bills that had gathered on the table beside her just to irritate him. 'Ah, yes, here it is. It's a pre-nup, isn't it?'

'You surely did not think I would marry you without protecting myself?'

'That depends on what sort of protection you're talking about.'

'This is a business deal, Nina, nothing more and nothing less.'

'Fine by me,' she said. 'As long as you don't try and go back on your word. How do I know if I can trust you?'

There was a brief but tense pause.

Nina imagined him grinding his teeth on the other end in an effort to maintain some sort of politeness and her stomach gave another funny little quiver.

'You will get your allowance as soon as the marriage is conducted and not a second before,' he bit out at last.

'Don't you trust me, Mr Marcello?' She used her sister's tone with relish. 'Do you think I might try and dupe you?'

'I would very much like to see you try,' he challenged her darkly. 'I am sure I do not have to warn you of the consequences if there is any double-dealing on your part.'

Nina couldn't help an inward shiver at the irony of his coolly delivered statement. As far as double-dealing went, hadn't she already dug her own grave?

'By the way,' he said, 'since we are marrying in a matter of days it is hardly appropriate for you to continue to call me by my surname.'

'Marc.' She breathed his name seductively. 'Is that short for Marco?'

'No, it is short for Marc,' he said. 'It is French, like my mother.'

'Do you speak French as well as Italian?'

'Yes, along with several other languages.'

She was privately impressed but wasn't going to acknowledge it to him.

'What about you?' he asked when she didn't immediately respond.

'Me?' She gave a quick snort. 'All that foreign rubbish? No way! English is the universal language, why anyone would bother chattering away in anything else is completely beyond me.'

She was more or less fluent in both his mother's tongue and in Italian, but had decided to keep it to herself. She'd studied languages at both school and tertiary level and enjoyed a certain level of proficiency. But it suited her purpose to let him think her a complete airhead who had nothing better to do than primp and preen to fill the time.

'I have made an appointment with my lawyer to meet us at

my office for us to sign the pre-nuptial agreement. You will also need to bring along your birth certificate so I can arrange the marriage licence,' he said. 'Is ten a.m. tomorrow convenient?'

Nina's heart started to pound with misgivings. Pretending to be her sister had been manageable to begin with, but now she was going to be signing binding documents in the presence of a lawyer. What if she were sent to prison for fraud? What would happen to Georgia then? Just as well she'd told him her real name was Nina, and even more fortunate she was the older twin, for only her name appeared on the document, making no mention of her twin as was the practice at the time. But what if he ever looked at Georgia's birth certificate? Nadia's name was printed there, not hers. How would she be able to explain that?

'Nina?' His deep voice interrupted her quiet panic.

'Sorry.' She hitched her niece a little higher on her hip. 'Georgia was slipping.'

'You are holding her?'

Just then Georgia gave a happy little gurgle as if she were responding to the sound of her uncle's voice.

'Yes,' Nina said, smiling down at her niece. 'I was about to put her back down for a sleep when you called.'

'How is she?'

'She's fine.'

'Does she wake much at night?'

'Once or twice,' she told him. 'But she soon settles back down.'

'Tell me something, Nina.' An indefinable quality entered his voice. 'Do you enjoy being a mother?'

Nina didn't hesitate in responding, 'Of course I do.'

There was a strange little silence.

She wondered if she should have been quite so honest. Perhaps Nadia would have answered completely differently and he was temporarily thrown by the sudden change of character.

'You do not strike me as the maternal type.' His tone was laced with scorn.

'What do I strike you as, Marc?' she asked in her most seductive voice, determined to make amends for her previous lapse in character.

Sitting in his office, Marc sighed, ignoring her last remark. 'I'll pick you up at nine-fifteen tomorrow,' he told her.

'Do you have a baby seat in your car?' she asked.

Marc frowned. He hadn't even thought about those sorts of details.

'I will have one fitted this afternoon.'

'I can catch a bus,' she offered. 'Where is your office?'

'I insist on picking you up.'

'I won't be going with you if your car isn't adequately fitted for carrying a child. It's not safe.'

Marc released his tight breath. 'I will have the seat fitted if it is the last thing I do, all right?'

'Good,' she said. 'Can I trust you on that?'

Marc closed his eyes and counted to ten.

'Marc?'

His eyes sprang open at the sound of his name on her lips. She had such a breathy voice, like a feather stroking along the sensitive skin on the back of his neck.

'Yes…' He cleared his throat. 'You can trust me.'

'I'll see you tomorrow then,' she said into the small silence.

'Yes.' Marc released his suddenly choking tie. 'See you tomorrow.'

The doorbell rang at nine-fifteen the next morning, but Georgia was still crying, as she had done from the moment she'd woken at five a.m.

Nina was getting desperate. She was already aching with tiredness, and the beginning of what promised to be a monumental headache was marshalling at the back of her eyes.

She gently patted Georgia's back as she answered the door, her hair hanging limply around her shoulders and her eyes hollow from lack of sleep.

When she saw the tall imposing figure of Marc Marcello

standing there it was all she could do to stop herself from howling in a similar vein to the small child in her arms.

'Is she sick?' Marc asked, stepping inside.

Nina brushed a long strand of hair out of her face and gave him an agonised look as the door closed behind him. 'I don't know. She's been like this from the moment she woke up.'

Marc took the baby from her, resting his open palm over the baby's forehead to check for a temperature.

'She is warm but not overly so.' He lifted his eyes back to Nina's. 'Has she had a feed?'

Nina shook her head. 'She turned away from it. I've offered it three or four times but she keeps pushing it away.'

'Maybe she needs to see a doctor,' he suggested. 'Who do you usually see?'

Nina looked at him blankly. For the life of her she couldn't think of who Nadia had taken Georgia to for her monthly check-ups, if indeed she had at all.

'I...'

Marc gave her an accusing look. 'You have taken her to a doctor, haven't you?'

'Ah...'

He let out his breath on a hiss of fury. 'This is a small child,' he railed at her. 'She is supposed to have regular jabs and weigh-ins to make sure she is growing to schedule.'

'She's perfectly healthy,' Nina said, wincing as Georgia let out another howl of misery.

Marc raised an accusing brow as the baby continued to cry in his arms. 'You think so?'

Nina bit her lip. 'Maybe she's teething.'

'She is how old? Four months? Isn't that a little early?'

'I don't know! I've never—' She stopped herself from saying the rest. How close she had been to telling him she knew nothing about babies! What sort of mother would he think her?

Marc had turned back to the infant, his strong capable hands stroking along Georgia's back as he held her. After a moment

or two the crying subsided to a few soft hiccups and after another minute or two the tiny eyelids fluttered closed.

Nina couldn't help admiring his technique. God knew she'd
been up for hours trying to get the baby to settle to no avail. A
part of her felt resentful that he'd achieved it instead of her.
Another part of her secretly admired him.

'Go and get ready.' Marc spoke to her in a lowered voice so
as not to disturb the child. 'We have a few minutes up our sleeves
but the traffic at this time of day is always an unknown variable.'

Nina made her way to her room and softly closed the door
behind her. She peered into the contents of her wardrobe with
dismay. Most of her clothes were either too conservative or out
of date. Her work as a librarian didn't require any degree of
fashionable attire, and as she'd so often had to bail her sister
out of debt she hadn't bought anything new for herself in ages.
She had jeans in abundance, mostly cast-offs from Nadia, and
a collection of tops, also from Nadia, most of which showed
far more than they concealed.

In the end she chose one of Nadia's cast-offs. She was supposed to be her sister so she figured she might as well dress
like her, even though she cringed at the thought of showing off
so much of her body, especially to someone so discerning of
female flesh as Marc Marcello.

Everything about him unsettled her. It wasn't just the fact
that he thought her to be her sister, although that in itself was
a major stumbling block, especially to her peace of mind, but
his whole manner seemed threatening in an overtly male sort
of way. Although she was aware that deep down he was acting
out of similar motives to her own, she couldn't help feeling on
edge around him. She knew some of it probably came from her
lack of experience with men; she just didn't know how to manage a man who was so strong, so in control and so determined.

Marc Marcello wasn't exactly the type of man one could ignore. He was the sort of man who was used to being obeyed—
insisted on it, in fact.

She sighed a little shakily as she straightened the close-fitting dress. She wished pretending to be her sister was as easy as putting on her twin's clothes: that way she wouldn't feel so nervous all the time in case he saw through her act. She snatched up a cashmere cardigan, slung it casually around her shoulders and made her way out to where Marc was waiting.

He was standing with the baby in his arms, the usually hard lines of his face soft as he gazed down at her sleeping form.

Nina drew in a painful breath at the sight before her. He clearly adored his brother's child and would do anything to protect her, even going so far as to marry a woman he loathed.

Marc turned to look at her and his expression instantly hardened. 'Are you ready?'

She nodded and, scooping up Georgia's changing bag, followed him out of the flat.

The trip to Marc's office was a silent one and Nina was immensely grateful for it. Georgia had finally accepted a bottle and fallen asleep not long after she'd been placed in the baby seat in the back of Marc's showroom-perfect car. Marc himself was concentrating on the thick morning traffic in front of him, his dark unreadable eyes looking straight ahead, his gaze never once veering her way.

Nina inspected her chewed nails for a moment as she considered what lay ahead. What had he told the lawyer about their sudden marriage? Was she supposed to pretend things were normal between them just like any other couple, or had Marc informed his lawyer of the particulars, Georgia of course being the primary one?

She curled her fingers into her palms and drew in a ragged breath.

Five words, she reminded herself. Five words and it could all end right here and now.

Sure, he'd have the power to remove Georgia from her custody, but maybe she'd be able to convince him to let her see her occasionally. Aunts had some sort of rights, didn't they? Not only that, she was also Georgia's godmother, although she'd never really understood why Nadia had bothered with the formality since the last time she had been in church was probably when she had been christened herself.

She sent him a covert glance but his head was turned towards the parking turnstile beneath the office tower he'd turned into, his hand reaching out of the driver's window to swipe his entry card.

The car surged forward as the boom rose and Nina turned back to face the front, not sure she wanted him to see the indecision and guilt written all over her face.

Once they were parked she got out of the car and began fitting the baby carrying pouch to her chest, her fingers almost shaking as she tried to fasten the buckle.

Marc handed Georgia to her, helpfully feeding the infant's legs through the appropriate holes. Nina felt the brush of his hand on her left breast and reared backwards as if he'd touched her with a heated brand.

His eyes met hers, the dark depths of his black gaze glittering with dislike.

'I would advise against any overt displays of distaste for my touch whilst we are in the presence of my lawyer,' he said. 'He believes this to be a normal marriage and I would prefer him to continue to do so in spite of what we both know privately to be true.'

Nina's eyes flashed as she adjusted the baby-carrier straps over her shoulders. 'It's not exactly normal to force someone to marry you.'

He activated the central locking and alarm system on his car before responding. 'You will be more than adequately compensated for your efforts.'

'Isn't the fact that I'm coming here to sign a pre-nuptial agreement going to make him suspicious?' she asked.

'Pre-nuptial agreements are commonplace these days.

Besides, I have shareholders and investors I need to protect, not to mention my father, who started the business from scratch. I will not stand by and watch a money-hungry little whore take half of all we have both worked so hard for if the marriage were to end.'

Although Nina knew everything he said was reasonable under the circumstances, she still felt hurt by his assessment of her motives. She wished he could see through her thin guise to the person she really was, not an opportunistic money-grabbing bed-hopping pleasure seeker, but a young woman who cared deeply for her tiny niece, so deeply, in fact, that she was prepared to marry a complete stranger.

She closed her mouth on her response and followed him into the lift he'd summoned. She stared fixedly at the numbers on the panel rather than look at him, but she was acutely aware of him standing beside her, his broad shoulder not quite touching hers, although she could feel the warmth of his body all the same.

The lift felt too small. Her chest felt too tight. Her legs felt like wet wool instead of toned muscle and bone. Her mind was a mess of disordered thoughts—thoughts of escape, thoughts of telling the truth, thoughts of what would happen if she went along with the lies she'd told, spending the rest of her life waiting for the axe to fall when the truth finally came out, as she knew it most certainly would.

So far she'd been lucky. He hadn't asked for Georgia's birth certificate, but it wouldn't be long before he did, particularly if he intended to formally adopt her. She knew he intended for his father to see his only grandchild, which would mean a trip to Italy. Would it even be legal for her to take Georgia out of the country? What if somebody asked to see the birth certificate and found out she wasn't in fact Georgia's mother? What then?

Suddenly conscious of Marc's probing gaze, she quickly covered her inner disquiet by plastering a vacant smile on her face.

'What are you smirking at?' Marc looked down at her derisively. 'How quickly you are going to work your way through your allowance?'

'That depends on how generous it is,' she tossed back.

Marc rolled his eyes and stabbed at the lift button once more as if to hurry its pace.

'We are not married yet so I would advise against counting your pennies until they have been dispatched,' he growled.

The lift doors sprang open and Nina followed the rigid line of his back as he made his way to his suite of offices.

It gave her a much needed sense of power to see how much she rattled him.

As far as she knew she had never got underneath anyone's skin before; that had always been Nadia's role, and yet the thought of Marc Marcello fighting an unwilling attraction to her was both strangely tantalizing and terrifying. She'd seen the way he'd looked at her when he'd thought she wasn't looking, his dark eyes lingering on her body as if he just couldn't help himself. It made her skin prickle all over in awareness to even think about him seeing her in such a light, let alone ever acting on it.

Her reaction to him totally confused her. She was supposed to hate him for what he was doing but somehow it wasn't quite working. Every time his eyes moved over her she felt as if he was transmitting heat from his body to hers. That brief accidental brush of his hand over her breast had felt like an electric shock, sending her pulse racing and her heart kicking in reaction.

She had to take better control, she mentally chided herself. To fall in love with Marc Marcello was asking for the sort of trouble she could well do without, considering the mess she was already in.

The reception area of Marc's banking empire could leave no one in any doubt of the company's considerable profits, Nina thought a short time later. From the sweeping computer console in the reception area fitted out in shining galaxy black marble, complete with a catwalk perfect receptionist, to the plush ankle-deep carpet on the floor, and the stunning views over the city from every window, it all left one with the impression that the Marcello merchant bank knew how to do business and do it extremely well.

Nina glanced towards a painting hung over the waiting room area, her eyes widening when she realized it wasn't a print but an actual Renoir.

'Mr Marcello,' the receptionist purred at her boss. 'Mr Highgate is waiting for you in the guest lounge adjoining your office.'

Nina's eyebrows rose. Even his lawyer thought the common waiting room beneath him, did he?

'Follow me,' Marc addressed Nina over one shoulder.

Something in her decided right there and then that she wasn't going to be ordered around in front of his staff, and in particular in front of his gorgeous receptionist, who had done nothing but stare at her the whole time she'd been there.

'Hello.' Nina held out her hand across the reception desk. 'I'm Nina, Marc's fiancée. And this is Georgia. She's Marc's niece, you know. Andre's child.'

The receptionist reared away from Nina's outstretched hand as if by touching it she might be fired on the spot.

'I…I thought your name was Nadia,' the young woman finally managed to get out. 'And don't you remember?' She eyeballed Nina accusingly. 'We've met before.'

Nina hadn't even considered the possibility that her sister might have called at the Marcello office tower at some stage in the past.

Her colour came and went as she tried to think of an excuse for not recognising the young woman but her brain felt as if someone had pulled the plug and she was left floundering.

'It was when Marc was in Italy last September,' the receptionist went on, her mouth tight with reproach. 'Andre was in a meeting but you insisted on seeing him.'

Nina was very aware of Marc listening to every word of this exchange and had to think on her feet to find a way out of it without blowing her cover.

Mentally counting back the months she realised Nadia must have come to see Andre well into the pregnancy, possibly as a last attempt to try to force his hand. She lowered her head in a gesture of contrition, her hand idly stroking the back of baby Georgia's head where she was snuggled up against her in the pouch.

'Yes…well, I wasn't really myself back then…hormones, you know…'

The receptionist peered over the console at the sleeping baby, her stern expression instantly softening. 'She's very like Andre, isn't she?'

Nina nodded, deciding it was probably wiser not to respond verbally even if she could have located her voice.

'Hold all my calls please, Katrina,' Marc's deep voice commanded, interrupting the tight little exchange. 'Come on, *cara*, we have some business to see to.'

Cara? Nina disguised her frown just in time. She wasn't sure she could handle him addressing her with Italian endearments. It made her feel as if their relationship was shifting to another level, a level she had no experience in dealing with.

She followed him down the spacious hall where even more priceless artworks were hung in stately array, each one reminding her of the amount of money Marc Marcello had at his fingertips if ever he decided to run her out of town—without Georgia.

'In here.' Marc held the door open for her. 'Take a seat and I will summon Robert Highgate to join us.'

Nina took one of the plush chairs facing the huge desk and, positioning Georgia into a more comfortable position against her, began to look around.

It was a huge office by anyone's standards. It was lined with bookshelves along two walls, the thick volumes rich with both a wealth of knowledge and variety of taste. Unless they were there simply for show, which somehow she seriously doubted, they indicated Marc was a man who read widely, for apart from the obvious financial and legal tomes she could see some recent bestsellers as well as some of the classics she'd read and loved herself.

It gave her a funny feeling to have read the same books as him. It gave her a connection with him she wasn't all that sure she wanted to have.

The door opened behind her and she turned in her seat to see a man of about fifty-five or so enter the room carrying a document folder under one arm. Marc was close behind with one of his impossible-to-read looks on his handsome face.

'*Cara*, this is Robert Highgate. Robert, this is my fiancée, Nina Selbourne.'

Nina began to rise but Robert hurriedly gestured for her to stay where she was on account of the baby nestled against her.

He shook her hand instead and looked down at the sleeping infant, his warm light brown eyes visibly softening.

'What a little treasure. I have two daughters of my own. They are both my life and my daily torture.' He grinned at her meaningfully.

Nina gave him a tentative smile. 'It's not easy being a parent.'

'No, but worth the struggle, I can assure you. My eldest is getting married in a few months; it seems only yesterday she was in ankle socks arguing with her mother over the length of her school uniform.'

Nina gave a somewhat forced little laugh. She had very clear memories of similar scenarios between Nadia and their mother but none of them were particularly amusing. She saw Marc stiffen at the sound of her chuckle, his dark eyes so piercing she had to look away in case he saw more than she wanted him to see.

'Now,' Robert said as he opened the folder on the desk and glanced across at Marc. 'I've drawn up the document the way you suggested but perhaps I should explain it to Nina first?'

'Explain away.' Marc's tone bordered on uninterested.

Nina felt herself shrinking in her seat in embarrassment. She had no real understanding of legal terms and wasn't sure if she'd be signing her life away. Surely the least Marc could do was go through it with her as well?

'As you wish.' Robert opened the file and laid it in front of her. 'Don't be put off by all the legalese, Nina, this is pretty straightforward. This simply states in the event of a divorce you agree to a reasonable settlement but not a division of Marc's total assets.'

Nina did her best to read through the wordy text but it made little if no sense to her. She kept searching the document for Georgia's name, hunting for some sort of clause Marc might have inserted to take the child away from her if the marriage was to fold, but as far as she could make out there was none.

'This bit here states that you will receive an allowance during your marriage.' Robert Highgate pointed to the relevant section.

Nina stared at the figure nominated there and swallowed. 'That seems a little…excessive.' She looked up and caught Marc looking at her strangely. She lowered her gaze to the documents once more, her heart pounding in her chest. She would have to be much more careful in future. Marc wasn't a fool. If he began to suspect he was being duped…

'If you could just sign here.' Robert Highgate indicated the dotted line for her. 'And over here.' He turned the page and she dutifully signed. 'There, that's all right and tight.' He closed the document and bundled it back in its folder as he turned to Marc, who was leaning against the filing cabinet behind his desk, his dark eyes still trained on her.

'May I offer you both my heartiest congratulations on a happy and fulfilling marriage?' Robert said. 'I know these are sad times but much joy can come about in spite of it.' He cleared his throat discreetly and added, 'How is your father, Marc?'

Marc pushed himself away from the filing cabinet. 'He's coping…just.'

Robert Highgate tut-tutted sympathetically, 'A terrible blow, and so soon after your mother.'

'Yes.'

Nina privately thought Marc's one word response spoke volumes. While he showed little emotion on his face, something in his voice suggested to her he was a man who felt deeply for all that. It made her see him in a new light. Not so much a hard-driven businessman who wanted to conquer the world, riding over people obstructing his way, but a man with a need to protect those he loved and felt responsible for.

He would make a wonderful father for Georgia.

The thought slipped into her mind and once in there took hold until she could think of nothing else. Visions of him with Georgia during her first Christmas, her first tooth, her first steps, her first day at school…her first boyfriend…

'What do you think, Nina?' Marc directed his gaze towards her.

Nina stared at him in blank confusion. 'Sorry?'

'Robert suggested we draw up a separate trust file on Georgia. Andre's estate now belongs to her, but until she comes of age—'

She got to her feet in sudden agitation, holding Georgia close to her chest to avoid disturbing her. 'I told you I'm not interested in Andre's estate.'

Marc sent her a quick warning glance but it was too late. Robert Highgate had seen the exchange and was at liberty to make his own conclusions.

'I'll have the necessary papers drawn up,' he informed Marc diplomatically as he reached for the door. 'Again, I wish you both well.'

'Thank you,' Marc said and, turning to Nina with an arch of one brow, prompted, 'Nina?'

She gave the lawyer a wan smile. 'Thank you, Mr Highgate, for explaining everything to me.'

'No problem.' Robert held out his hand and grasped hers firmly. 'You know you're nothing like I thought you'd be, if you don't mind me saying.'

'I—I'm not?' Nina's stomach rolled over. God, had Nadia met him too at some stage?

'No,' Robert said. 'But then you know what those gossip columns are like; they make that stuff up to sell the next magazine.'

Nina's heart instantly sank. She shifted uncomfortably from foot to foot as she tortured herself with images of her scantily clad sister cavorting at God knew which of Sydney's nightclubs in order to have her photo plastered over some seedy gossip page.

She lowered her gaze to the child in her arms and affected a demure pose. 'That's all behind me now. I'm a changed person.'

'I congratulate you for it,' Robert Highgate said. 'Bringing up a child is a very maturing experience. Do you have any family—parents and so on?'

She shook her head, carefully avoiding his eyes. 'No, no family. My father died when I was a baby and my mother died three years ago.'

Marc frowned as he listened to the exchange between his lawyer and his soon-to-be wife. He suddenly realised how little he knew of Nina and her background. He knew she was known to be an unprincipled whore who had made it her life's goal to hunt down a rich husband to set her up for life, but he hadn't known she had grown up without a father and had so recently lost her mother. His own grief reminded him of how devastating losing a parent could be and something inside him shifted a little ground. Yes, she was undoubtedly an opportunist and she sure as hell had driven his brother to his untimely end...but she clearly loved Georgia, which still somehow surprised him.

The door closed behind the lawyer and Georgia began to

grizzle. Nina extracted her from the baby-carrier and, reaching for the nappy bag, looked across at Marc who was standing in a brooding silence behind his desk.

'I think she needs her nappy changed,' she said.

'Would you like me to do it?' he offered.

Nina stared at him in silent horror for a moment. How could she let him change Georgia's nappy with the faint smudge of bruises still on her tiny chest?

'No,' she said flatly.

Something came and went in his eyes and she knew she had offended him. He wanted to be a father to Georgia, a real and involved father who would feed and change a baby without rearing away in distaste as some men would do. But until those bruises were gone she had no choice but to keep him well away from Georgia without the shield of her clothes.

'There is a bathroom two doors down,' he said, moving from behind the desk. 'Do you have what you need with you?'

Nina gave him an imperious look as she held up the well-stocked nappy bag. 'I have done this before, you know.'

Marc didn't answer but he held the door open for her as she stalked past him with her head held high. He watched as she made her way down the corridor to where the bathroom was situated, Georgia snuggled on one of her slim hips, the baby's tiny hands buried in the length of her shiny blonde hair.

His own fingers itched to do the same, to see if it was really as silky as it looked, but with a silent curse he thrust his hands deep into his trouser pockets and let the office door click shut as he went back his desk.

He ignored his chair and instead turned to look out of the window as he had done thousands of times before, but this time he saw nothing of the harbour.

All he could see was a pair of smoky grey eyes.

CHAPTER FIVE

Nina took as long as she could in the bathroom seeing to Georgia's needs. She needed time to think. So much was happening and happening so fast she hadn't had time to get her head into gear.

She felt a fool for not anticipating people such as Marc's receptionist having met her sister previously. And no doubt there would be other people she'd have to pretend she knew. And that little slip about the allowance— Oh, God! Her stomach clenched with tight fingers of fear as she thought of her charade coming unstuck in such a way.

She daredn't even think about Marc's reaction.

He turned from the window when she returned to his office and, in spite of her determination to keep cool and calm under pressure, she couldn't help a tiny flip-flop in her belly at the sheer height and presence of him as he came towards her.

'It has occurred to me that there are quite probably things Georgia needs, such as new clothing or toys,' he said, taking the baby from her with gentle hands. 'I have some time available now, so we could go shopping if you like.'

Nina stared up at him, uncertain of how to answer.

Georgia was in desperate need of clothes as she was growing so fast, but shopping with Marc as if they were any normal couple…?

She lowered her gaze and pretended to be re-sorting the changing bag to avoid looking directly at him as she hunted her brain for some sort of excuse.

'Since your own clothes are designer labels, surely your child is entitled to the same?' A hard edge had crept into his voice.

Nina tensed as she pushed the lid back down on the baby wipes container. She'd picked up one of Nadia's cast-offs thinking it was one of the more conservative of the collection she'd left behind, never dreaming it was actually haute couture.

'This old thing?' she quipped with a disdainful glance down at the cashmere she was wearing.

Marc's mouth curled. 'I suppose you only wear an outfit once before it is thrown to the back of the wardrobe?'

Nina almost laughed at how close he was to describing her sister's attitude to clothes. She could have afforded designer wear herself if she'd been given a dollar for every time she'd picked some discarded article up off the floor after one of Nadia's wild nights out.

She tossed her long hair behind one shoulder and smiled up at him saucily. 'Is it my fault I get bored easily?'

'You know something, Nina Selbourne?' He gave her a cutting look. 'I am almost looking forward to being married to you so I can teach you how to behave. You are the shallowest young woman I have ever had the misfortune to meet. I think it will be a great pleasure to bring you to heel as someone should have done a very long time ago.'

Nina pretended to shudder in trepidation. 'Oh! I am *sooo* scared of you, Mr Marcello.'

His black eyes glittered with contempt. 'If I was not holding Georgia right at this minute I would be tempted to begin lesson one right here and now,' he bit out.

Nina's eyes flashed at him with false bravado. 'You lay one finger on me and you will be the poorer for it.'

'It would be worth it, I can assure you,' he shot back.

'You think?' She tilted her chin at him. 'Your brother certainly thought so.'

Nina knew the only thing that saved her at that point was the fact that Georgia was in his arms. Her tiny starfish hands were clutching at the stark whiteness of his business shirt, her little elfin face looking up at him as if in wonder, her brown-black eyes so like his own with their thick fringe of lashes.

Nina saw the struggle he had to control himself playing out on his features as he stood before her. The line of his mouth was grim, his jaw tight with suppressed anger and his eyes sparking at her as if he wanted to torch her to the ground right then and there.

The intercom on his desk broke the brittle silence.

'Mr Marcello?' Katrina's cheerful tone entered the room like a light being switched on in pitch blackness. 'Your father is on line two.'

Marc handed Georgia back to Nina without meeting her eyes. 'Excuse me.' He turned his back to attend to the call.

Nina reached with one hand for the baby pouch where she'd left it earlier when she heard the first few words of Marc's conversation with his father. Even though he spoke his native tongue rapidly she had studied the language long enough to pick up on the general gist of the exchange.

'Yes,' Marc said. 'I have found a solution. I am marrying her on the fifteenth.'

Nina couldn't hear what his father said in response but she could more or less piece together the rest on Marc's reply.

'No, she insists she does not want any money or anything to do with Andre's estate... I am not sure but I suspect she is trying to butter me up by pretending to be a changed person... Yes, I have arranged an allowance but it will not take her long to work her way through that, I am sure... Yes, I know she is everything that Andre said and more... I know, I know...she is an unprincipled whore...'

Nina had trouble keeping her reaction disguised. She silently fumed and vowed revenge on his insulting assessment of her as she eased Georgia back into the pouch.

'Yes…I know, I will watch my back, and yes…' Marc gave a distinctly male chuckle '…my front as well. *Ciao.*'

Nina smiled guilelessly as she turned back to face him. 'So, where are we going shopping?'

A short time later, as they began trawling the department stores as well as exclusive designer boutiques, Nina had cause to wonder if she had catapulted herself into some sort of shopaholic's dream. Marc's credit card was flashed so many times she thought she was going to go blind with the amount of currency going past her eyes as he bought item after item for his niece. Beautiful clothes, expensive toys, special feeder cups for when she came off her bottle—all were parcelled off to be delivered to his office.

When it was time for Georgia's next feed Marc suggested they go to a quiet café where she could feed the baby whilst they had a coffee and a sandwich.

Nina wished she wasn't starving so she could refuse, but she'd missed breakfast due to Georgia's crying bout and her stomach was letting her know in no uncertain terms it was well and truly time for a pit stop.

They were soon seated in a booth in a café overlooking the lively shopping mall below. The rushing lunchtime crowds and talented buskers performing below added to the high energy of the city.

Georgia's bottle was soon heated and brought back to the table by a young waitress. Once she'd gone, Nina was about to offer her niece the bottle when she caught Marc's dark gaze on her.

'Would you like to feed her?' she found herself asking him.

His dark eyes held hers for a brief moment of silent hesitation.

'Sure, why not?' he finally answered and, standing up, reached across the table to gather Georgia in his arms.

Once he was seated, Nina handed him the bottle and a soft cloth she used to catch any drips. She leaned back in her own seat and watched as he positioned the teat for Georgia's searching mouth.

Seeing the way he held the child set off a funny reaction deep inside Nina's belly, like the sudden unfurling of a tightly wound ball of string. She shifted in her seat and forced herself to look at the menu the waitress had left for their perusal but the words all seemed a blur to her as her thoughts shot off in all directions.

Marc was so at ease handling his niece and she wondered if he had ever wanted children of his own. If so, why was he tying himself to her in a loveless paper marriage?

She knew Italians had a deep sense of family, and the value of children in their lives was high. But surely marrying a stranger, even though she was supposedly the mother of his brother's child, was going a little too far in terms of familial duty?

It had occurred to her that he might annul the marriage at some point in the future and apply for full custody of Georgia. It was an uncomfortable scenario as she knew she wouldn't stand a chance once her true identity became known. She would be seen as a scheming, manipulating liar and no magistrate would hand her niece to her, even for access visits, let alone assign her full or partial custody.

Suddenly her earlier gnawing hunger faded and she pushed the menu away with a slump of her shoulders.

'Not hungry?' Marc's eyes met hers across the table.

'I'll just have coffee.' She shifted her gaze from his. 'Black.'

The waitress came over and took the order from Marc, lingering to hover over the baby who had by now finished her bottle.

'How old is she?' the young girl asked.

'Four months,' Nina answered.

The waitress smiled as she looked between the baby and Marc. 'She's like her daddy, isn't she?'

It was on the tip of Nina's tongue to say that Marc wasn't actually Georgia's father but something stopped her at the last minute.

'Yes,' she said instead, shocked that she hadn't seen it before now.

Georgia did have a look of Marc about her, seemingly more so as each day passed. Her olive colouring was one thing, so too the dark eyes and silky black hair. But she could also see evidence of herself and Nadia in the rosebud mouth and the slightly *retroussé* nose and wondered if he could too.

The waitress bustled off to get their coffee and Nina watched as Marc eased Georgia up against his shoulder, gently patting her tiny back as if he'd done it a hundred times before.

'Have you given any thought to having a child of your own some time in the future?' she asked before she could stop herself.

Marc's expression gave little away but Nina was sure she saw a flicker of regret pass through his dark-as-night eyes before he quickly disguised it.

'No.' He shifted Georgia to his other shoulder. 'I had not planned on marrying and doing the whole family-rearing thing.'

His answer intrigued her. She knew there were plenty of sworn-in life members of bachelordom about the place, but somehow Marc didn't seem the type.

'Was this your father's idea for us to marry?'

His eyes met hers, holding her questioning gaze intently. 'What makes you say that?'

'I…' She fiddled with the edge of the tablecloth, doing her best to avoid the full force of his all-seeing eyes. 'A hunch, I guess. I've heard Italians are pretty big on kids.'

'I suppose that is why you sent him that letter to twist the knife a bit,' he said, leaning forwards on the table so the other diners couldn't hear his harsh accusation. 'Did you ever consider how much you were hurting an elderly man who is already doing his best to cope with unbearable grief?'

Nina wished she could tell him the truth. It hurt so much to have him think so poorly of her when in fact it had been her sister who had acted so unthinkingly.

'No.' She let the edge of the tablecloth go and raised her eyes to his condemning ones. 'No, it was very insensitive of me. I'm sorry.'

Her answer seemed to surprise him. If it had come from Nadia, it would have surprised even her, Nina thought wryly. She couldn't recall a single time when her sister had apologised for anything; 'I'm sorry' just wasn't in her twin's vocabulary.

'Sometimes sorry is not enough,' he said, leaning back again, settling Georgia more comfortably against his shoulder. 'Once the damage is done there is no going back to undo it.'

Nina felt sick at the truth of his curt statement. How much damage had she already done with all the lies she'd been forced to tell on her sister's behalf?

'Yes, I know.' She stared at the salt and pepper shakers standing side by side like small china soldiers on the table in front of her. 'I guess I was so confused at the time… I hardly knew what I was doing.'

There was a small silence broken only by the soft gurgling of Georgia, who had found the breast pocket of Marc's business shirt, her tiny fingers clutching at the fabric in delight.

'You deliberately tried to trap my brother, did you not?' he upbraided her. 'By using the oldest trick in the book.'

She wished she could deny it on Nadia's behalf but knew that too would be yet another lie. Her sister had deliberately set about to snare Andre Marcello by fair means or foul. Nina had been appalled when Nadia had told her of her plan to trap him, casually revealing the way she'd sabotaged a whole box of condoms in order to bring about a pregnancy as if it was all a game, not real life with the potential for irreparable damage to occur. Nina still tortured herself with her own guilt at not being able to talk her sister out of it. Maybe if she'd spent more time with her, had counselled her to think a little further ahead than the next moment of pleasure…

'It was a stupidly impulsive thing to do...' she finally said, her voice low, her eyes downcast. 'I had no idea of how it would backfire on...me.'

Again her answer seemed to surprise him. She chanced a look at him and found his hard accusatory expression had softened slightly as he looked across at her, the child in his arms nestling against him preparatory to sleep.

'There are few of us who get through life without one or two regrets,' he offered.

Nina gave him a rueful smile. 'Don't tell me the great Marc Marcello admits to getting it wrong now and again?'

He held her gaze for a moment before looking down at the child in his arms. 'I have made one or two errors of judgement in the past but I have no intention of ever doing so again.'

Nina wondered if he bore the internal scars of a broken relationship which had made him wary of emotional commitment. The more she thought about it, the more likely it seemed. What better way to take himself out of the game than to marry for convenience, not love? He would be free to liaise with whomever he chose without the pressure of formal commitment due to the piece of paper that would soon be documenting her as his wife.

His wife...

She swallowed a lump of panic as she thought about all such a relationship would entail. Even though he'd stated implacably that the marriage would not be consummated, they would still be living in the same house which would force certain intimacies on them both regardless.

She imagined seeing him in less formal attire, perhaps in sports gear or after a shower with a towel around his waist, his long strong body exposed. Or seeing him unshaven in the morning, his chiselled jaw dark with stubbly growth, the sort of growth that tingled female skin if it brushed up against it...

Nina pulled back from her thoughts with a little jerk in her chair, her guilty glance meeting Marc's questioning one.

'Is something wrong?' he asked.

'No, of course not.'

'You do not seem yourself,' he observed.

'Oh, really?' She gave him one of Nadia's scathing looks. 'And you know me so well after, what is it—' She checked her watch for the date and looked back at him. 'Less than a week?'

'Suffice it to say I am familiar with your type,' he answered smoothly.

'So you think one size fits all?'

His smile was cynically lopsided. 'I have been around long enough to recognise danger when I see it.'

'Danger, eh?' She arranged her lips into a smirk. 'You see me as dangerous? What exactly are you threatened by? My sex appeal?'

His mouth tightened and she knew she'd scored another hit. It struck her as ironic that he was fighting an attraction to her when she was pretending to be someone else. What chance did she stand of him being attracted to her as Nina—the *real* Nina? The Nina without the reputation or the Nina without the baggage? Not to mention the Nina without the designer wardrobe. The Nina who was in very great danger of falling in love with a man who despised the very sight of her.

'Your ego no doubt has had considerable stroking over the years but I refuse to join your band of avid admirers,' he said. 'If you are looking for compliments I am afraid you will have to go elsewhere.'

Nina gave him an arch look. 'But you do find me attractive, don't you? Go on, admit it.'

'I admit nothing.'

She laughed. 'You'll get sand in your eyes if you bury your head too deeply.'

She saw his jaw tighten another notch. 'Women like you think they are irresistible but let me tell you, you are not. Do you think I am so easily swayed by full breasts and pouting lips and come-to-bed eyes?'

She pursed the said pouting lips and affected a super-confident pose. 'I can *feel* your interest from right over here,' she said in a breathy undertone. 'I bet if I slipped my hand under this table and examined the evidence for myself you'd have some serious back-pedalling to do.'

Black eyes met grey in a challenge that rocked Nina to her very core but she was determined not to back down. She held his look with a spirited defiance she hadn't thought herself capable of.

Although he tried to disguise it, she noticed he shifted backwards in his chair as if he didn't trust her not to do exactly as she'd said. Her mind began to wander of its own volition... What would he feel like fully aroused? Would he shudder at the touch of her fingers around his length or would he groan with deep out of control pleasure? And what would his reaction be if her mouth were to close over him, drawing from him a response that would spill his life force out of his body in an explosion of pleasure?

'It's time to leave.' His announcement was curt as he got stiffly to his feet.

Georgia gave a soft rumble of protest about the sudden movement but soon settled back against his chest, her tiny eyelids fluttering closed, her miniature fingers still grasping his breast pocket.

Nina rose with less speed, taking her time to gather up the baby's changing bag and her own handbag, shooting him a glance from across the width of the table.

'Do you think it's worth disturbing her to put her back in the pouch?' she asked.

Marc looked down at the tiny infant against his chest and shook his head. 'No.' He lifted his gaze back to hers. 'I will carry her.' He scooped up the bill the waitress had left and added, 'Is there anything else we need to buy?'

It was the 'we' that really got to her. Seeing him with Georgia cradled so tenderly in his arms, she couldn't help feeling a deep sense of regret over how circumstances had led them both to this. How different things might have been if they had met without the baggage of both of their wayward siblings. If the truth were known they probably had more in common than not. He was the solid dependable type, anyone could see that, and she…well, she was hardly the sleep-around town tart he thought her to be.

If only he knew!

'No.' She carefully avoided his eyes in case he saw the glitter of sudden moisture. 'I think we're more or less done.' She hoisted the changing bag over her shoulder and followed him out of the café with her head well down.

The city streets were so busy as to make conversation both difficult and unnecessary. Nina was glad of the reprieve. Guilt flooded her from every direction. Maybe she should have been firmer with Nadia, should have insisted she stay and face her responsibilities. But then, when had Nadia ever faced anything? Her policy had been to move from one disaster to the next with her twin picking up the pieces behind her. Nina had even done it for their mother in the past, becoming the parent instead of the child in an attempt to provide some level of security for them. Much good it had done in the end, she thought sadly. Her mother had still drunk and drugged herself into an early grave and there had been nothing Nina could do to stop it.

Marc pressed the pedestrian button and flicked a glance down at the silent figure beside him as they waited for the lights to change. 'You are very quiet all of a sudden.'

Nina shook herself out of her mental anguish and sent a vacant smile his way. 'I'm just tired.' She yawned widely. 'Georgia woke me early.' She patted her mouth and forced another smile. 'Kids; who in their right mind would have them?'

Marc was saved a reply by the lights changing. It was clear to him that money was Nina's primary motive and she had targeted the richest man she could and had got on with the business of falling pregnant to him. But it was still somewhat of a mystery to him why she hadn't asked for a whole heap of money when he'd offered her marriage. He'd been expecting her price to be in the millions and yet even the allowance he'd organised for her had seemingly surprised her. And, as for pretending she had no interest in Andre's estate, what possible reason could she have other than to try and fool him into thinking she had somehow changed from a money-hungry pleasure seeker to a woman of high morals?

But he knew Nina was trouble from the top of her shiny head to the soles of her dainty feet. She had a disturbing habit of switching from sultry siren to wide-eyed innocent as if she was deliberately trying to confuse him about who she really was. If Andre hadn't told him how manipulative she was he would sometimes be tempted to think he was dealing with someone else entirely.

He slanted a covert glance her way, instantly noting the line of her slightly anxious brow and the way her small white teeth nibbled at her bottom lip.

He gave a rough inward sigh. Marrying her was going to be the easy part; however, he was starting to think that if he wasn't very careful, keeping his hands off her was going to be something else indeed.

CHAPTER SIX

ONCE Nina was confident there was no trace of Georgia's bruises remaining she arranged to return to work. However, when she made to leave the childcare centre the following day, her tiny niece howled miserably, her little arms reaching out to her from the carer's hold.

'Don't worry, Miss Selbourne,' the childcare worker reassured her. 'She'll settle down once you leave. They all do.'

Nina bit her lip in an agony of indecision. Georgia's little face was bright red, her eyes spilling tears and her desperate wails increasing in volume.

'Maybe I should call work and tell them I can't make it.'

'Of course you shouldn't,' the woman said. 'She'll be fine. I'll take her to look at the toys while you leave. Feel free to phone as soon as you get to work but I am sure you've got nothing to worry about. Come on, Georgia,' she told the child with a smile. 'Let's go and look at the nice teddy bears over here.'

Nina could still hear Georgia's cries as she made her way outside the building, her heart squeezing painfully at the thought of her niece being so upset at the prospect of being abandoned. It made her realise anew how important it was to protect her, for it was obvious the baby considered her to be her primary carer. If Marc were to find out who she really was now, Georgia would be the one to suffer, for Nina felt sure he would evict her from the child's life as soon as he possibly could.

The library was a few blocks away and she walked there with dragging steps, wondering how mothers across the globe dealt with leaving their children in someone else's care.

She loved her job but she loved her niece more. If push came to shove she would have to quit work, swallow her pride and accept the allowance from Marc that his lawyer had arranged in the pre-nuptial agreement.

'Hi, Nina,' Elizabeth Loughton, one of the other librarians, greeted her as soon as she arrived at work. 'Hey, where have you been the last few days? Sheila said you called in sick. Are you OK now?'

Nina placed her bag in the staffroom locker in order to avoid her friend's probing look. 'I'm fine, just a bit tired. It's been one of those weeks.'

'Don't tell me your sister has been giving you trouble again,' Elizabeth said. 'I don't know why you don't tell her where to get off, really I don't. She takes advantage of you so much, no wonder you're not well.' She pursed her lips for a moment, then, moving over to close the staffroom door, turned back and handed Nina a recent edition of a popular gossip magazine. 'I suppose you've already seen this?'

Nina disguised a gulp as she looked down at the magazine article Elizabeth had shown her. There was a photograph of her twin outside one of Sydney's best known hotels, dressed in a revealing dress that left little to the imagination, her arms flung around the necks of two well known football personalities who both had dubious reputations with regard to their treatment of women. The caption hinted that, according to hotel staff sources, last Friday night Nadia and her male escorts had engaged in a drunken noisy threesome upstairs.

'Oh, God.' She shut the magazine and handed it back as they sat down together. 'This is just what I don't need right now.'

'Are you all right?' Elizabeth peered at her in concern.

Nina met her friend's hazel gaze. 'I have to tell you something but you have to promise not to tell anyone else.'

Elizabeth used a finger to zip her lips. 'Mum's the word.'

Nina's mouth twisted wryly. 'That's exactly right. Mum *is* the word you now have to use when referring to me.'

Elizabeth's eyes went out on stalks. 'Oh, my God! You're pregnant?'

Nina rolled her eyes. 'Of course not! No, but I am now acting as Georgia's mother.'

As Nina filled her in on previous events, Elizabeth's face fell in horror.

'Are you completely nuts?' Elizabeth had got to her feet in agitation. 'What the hell are you thinking? This Marc Marcello will eat you alive when he finds out! You could go to prison or something!'

'What else can I do?' Nina asked. 'Georgia needs me. Nadia was going to give her up for adoption but this way I can keep her and give her the love she deserves. It's a small price to pay.'

'A small price?' Elizabeth gaped at her. 'What do you know about this guy?'

Nina couldn't help a tiny smile. 'I know he adores Georgia and she adores him.'

'And what about you?' Elizabeth gave her another probing look. 'What does he feel about you? Does he adore you too?'

'No.' Nina lowered her gaze.

There was a short silence and Nina looked up to see her friend's contemplative gaze trained on her.

'I think I'm starting to get the picture,' Elizabeth said. 'You're in love with him, aren't you?'

'How could I possibly be in love with him?' Nina's eyes darted away once more. 'I hardly know him.'

'You must feel something for him because, knowing you as I do, you would never agree to marry someone if you didn't respect and admire them at the very least.'

Nina thought about it for a moment. Yes, she did respect Marc. In fact, if circumstances were different, he was exactly the sort of man she could come to love. He had qualities she couldn't help admiring. He was fiercely loyal and protective and his sense of family was strong.

'Come on, Nina,' Elizabeth continued. 'I can see it in your eyes. You're halfway there already.'

'You're imagining things.'

'Maybe I am, but I'd watch it if I were you,' Elizabeth cautioned. 'You're not the hard-nosed bitch your sister is. You are going to get yourself seriously hurt if you don't take care.'

'I know what I'm doing,' Nina said. 'Anyway, I don't have a choice. I love Georgia and would do anything to protect her.'

'Sounds like you and that future husband of yours have rather a lot in common, don't you think?' Elizabeth mused as she opened the staffroom door. 'You both want the same thing and are prepared to go to extraordinary lengths to get it.'

Nina didn't answer. She was starting to think it might have been a mistake to tell Elizabeth the truth about her situation. Her friend was seeing things Nina herself had pointedly refused to examine too closely.

She turned to the phone on the wall and quickly called the childcare centre to check on her niece, relieved to hear that Georgia had finally fallen asleep. She hung up the phone and made her way out to the front desk, glad she had something to do other than think about Marc Marcello and how she really felt about him.

Nina had not long returned home with Georgia later that day when the phone rang.

'Nina?' Her sister's voice sounded in her ear. 'Is that you?'

'Who else would it be?' Nina said tersely.

Nadia laughed. 'Well, for a minute there I thought you sounded just like me.'

Nina ground her teeth. 'That is *so* not funny. You do realise that all because of your stupid actions I will be marrying Andre's brother in a matter of days, don't you?'

'Lucky you,' Nadia said. 'I'm sure you'll be more than adequately compensated. A billionaire to call your own.'

'His money means nothing to me,' she bit out.

'Good,' Nadia said. 'Then you won't mind sending it to me.'

'What?' Nina stiffened.

'Come on, Nina. You'll be loaded. We talked about this the other day, remember? I expect you to share your good fortune with me. Besides, we're sisters, twin sisters.'

Nina drew in a breath. 'I am *not* taking his money.'

'Don't be stupid; he's giving it to you in exchange for marriage. You have to take it.'

'I have no intention of doing so.'

'Listen.' Nadia's voice hardened. 'If you don't take it I'll tell him who you really are.'

Nina swallowed, her hand on the receiver growing white-knuckled. 'You can't do that. He'll take Georgia off me.'

'Do you think I care?' Nadia said.

'How can you be so callous?' Nina cried. 'You're her mother, for God's sake!'

'If you don't take the money and give it to me I will tell him how you've deceived him. Somehow I don't think he'll take all that kindly to the news.'

Nina could well believe it, but this wasn't about her at all. It was about Georgia. She loved her niece and couldn't bear the thought of never seeing her again.

She considered going to Marc and telling him the truth before Nadia got the chance but knew in the end it would be pointless. He would simply remove Georgia from her custody, would no doubt be relieved that he didn't have to bind himself to her after all. He would have no regard for her feelings as the child's aunt even if she was to plead with him to allow her a place in Georgia's life.

'I haven't got any money yet,' Nina said. 'The marriage doesn't take place for another few days. Marc told me I won't get the allowance until the ink dries on the marriage certificate.'

'Well, when it does I want you to send me it. All of it. I'll give you my bank details.'

Nina put the phone down a few minutes later, the numbers on the piece of paper in her hand making her feel sick to her stomach.

Her sister had just sold her child.

CHAPTER SEVEN

NINA had not long settled Georgia for the night when the doorbell rang. She didn't have to check through the peephole; she knew it was Marc by the way her skin had started to tingle all over.

She opened the door and stepped aside to allow him to come in, her tone reproving as she said, 'You should have called to say you were going to visit. Georgia's just gone down. I don't want to unsettle her.'

'I am not here to see Georgia right now,' Marc said, closing the door behind him.

Nina tucked a strand of wayward hair behind one ear and did her best to hold his unwavering gaze. 'W-what did you want to see me about?'

'Where were you today?' he asked.

'Um…why do you ask?'

'I called you for hours but you didn't answer.'

'I am allowed to go out, aren't I?' She gave him a hardened look. 'Or is my being a prisoner part of your stipulations?'

'No, but I would prefer it if you would keep me informed of where you and Georgia will be in case I need to contact you. Do you have a mobile phone?'

'Yes, but I don't have it on a lot as it wakes Georgia,' she said half truthfully.

'I have something else I would like to discuss with you,' he added and, reaching into his coat pocket, took out the magazine Elizabeth had shown her that morning.

She took it from him with unsteady fingers and placed it on the coffee table without opening it to the damning page.

'I take it you have already seen it?' he said.

'Yes.'

'And?'

She met his diamond-hard gaze. 'That was more than a week ago. Besides, you know how these magazines like to blow things out of proportion.'

'Did you sleep with those men?'

Nina's stomach quivered at the steely edge to his tone but she forced herself to respond with a steadiness she was nowhere near feeling. 'No.'

'You lying little—' His mouth snapped shut as if he felt tainted by even uttering the rest of the vilifying sentence.

'I am not lying,' she stated quietly.

His jaw tightened and his hands went to fists at his sides. 'I am going to ask you again where you were today and I expect you to tell me the truth.'

'I went to the library.'

'The library?'

She lifted her chin and folded her arms across her chest. 'Yes, it's this really boring place full of books where you have to be quiet all the time. I thought I'd check it out, you know, to improve my mind a bit.'

'You went there all day?' He looked sceptical.

'For a big part of it,' she answered. 'That's why my phone was switched off. What did you do all day?'

'I was working.'

'Oh, really?' She gave him an equally sceptical look. 'Can you prove it?'

He frowned at her. 'I do not have to prove anything to you.'

She tilted her head at him. 'Nor do I to you.'

'If I find out you are lying to me, Nina, you will be very sorry.'

'I don't have to answer to you until we are married,' she said. 'And even then I will not tolerate you bossing me around as if I don't have a mind of my own. Now, if you have finished discussing what you came here to discuss, I think you should leave.'

'I will leave when I am good and ready.' He closed the small distance between them, one of his hands going to the wall at the side of her head, his eyes holding hers as his body pressed close.

Too close.

Nina felt the sharp nudge of desire his sudden closeness evoked, her legs weakening beneath her and her heart thumping erratically behind the wall of her chest. Her breasts seemed to swell as she pressed her back against the wall, the spicy fragrance of his aftershave teasing her nostrils as he leaned even closer.

'P-please go away.' Her voice came out choked.

She felt herself drowning in the fathomless depth of his dark eyes. The silence stretched and stretched until she could hear a faint ringing in her ears. She wondered if he was going to kiss her and her gaze instinctively flicked to his mouth, her heart doing another funny kick-start at the thought of those sensual lips pressed to hers.

Her eyes returned to his and instantly widened as she began to feel the metal of his belt buckle against her stomach and the potent strength of what she could feel was stirring just below. She could feel the energy of his body sending a charge of crackling electricity to hers, making her flesh prickle all over with sensory alertness.

She drew in a shaky breath, her breasts rising and falling against his chest as her heart began to race. His eyes dipped to her mouth, lingering there for endless pulsing seconds before he lifted his hand and traced the contour of her bottom lip with the blunt pad of his thumb, back and forth, slowly, tantalizingly.

Just when she thought she could stand it no longer, he dropped his hand from her mouth and stepped back from her, his expression closing over.

'I will see you tomorrow. What time would be convenient for me to call around?'

It took her several seconds to get her brain back into gear. 'Um…about this time is good. I'll be out all day.'

He gave her a wry look as he reached for the door. 'The library again?'

'Yes…I thought I might read some books to Georgia. It's supposed to be good for language development.'

He looked as if he was going to say something but apparently changed his mind at the last minute. Nina watched as he opened the door and stepped through, casting her one last inscrutable look as he shut it behind him.

She stared at the door while she waited for her heart rate to return to normal.

Elizabeth was right, she thought as she let out a little uneven breath. As far as falling for Marc Marcello went, she was more than halfway there already.

Georgia was even worse the next morning when Nina tried to leave the childcare centre. The pitiful cries shredded her nerves and, even though the assistant was just as reassuring and confident as the day before, Nina felt the full weight of her guilt drag her down as she made her way to the front door, her eyes stinging with the threat of tears.

She didn't see the tall figure leaning against his car near the front entrance until it was too late. She came to a stumbling halt as Marc's shadow blocked out the watery sunlight, her heart leaping towards her throat.

'M-Marc…what are you doing here?'

'I could ask you the very same thing but I already know the answer.' His dark gaze flicked to the childcare signage behind her. 'So this is where you relieve yourself of your responsibilities towards Georgia, no doubt so you can cavort all day with your lovers.'

'No…*no!* It's not like that at all.'

One dark brow rose in cynicism. 'Perhaps you would like to explain to me why you have placed my niece in the care of complete strangers.'

'They're not exactly strangers,' Nina said. 'They're highly competent childcare workers.'

His mouth tightened as he took her by the arm. 'Then we will go and see just how competent they are, shall we?'

Nina had no choice but to follow him for his hold, though loose, was under-wired with steely determination. She could feel the latent strength in his long fingers as they circled her wrist.

It wasn't hard for him to find where Georgia was being looked after. Her cries were echoing throughout the building. As they approached the babies' room Nina felt the tightening of Marc's hold as if his anger was travelling through his body to where it was joined to hers.

'There, there, Georgia,' the childcare assistant was cooing as she cuddled her. 'Mummy will be back later…now, now, don't cry…Oh, hello again, Miss Selbourne,' she said as she turned around. 'I'm afraid your little girl is not settling all that well this morning.'

Nina took Georgia from the woman's arms and the howling stopped immediately, to be replaced by tiny hiccups and sniffles as the baby clung to her.

'That's all right,' Nina said. 'I don't think I will leave her today, after all.'

'We can try again tomorrow, if you like,' the woman suggested. 'As I said the other day, lots of babies find separation from mum hard at first but they soon get used to it.'

'Miss Selbourne will not need your services any more,' Marc announced in clipped tones. 'We have made other arrangements.'

The woman's eyebrows rose slightly and Nina hastily inserted, 'This is my...fiancé, Marc Marcello.'

'Oh...well, then...' The woman gave a slightly flustered smile.

'Come on, *cara*.' Marc took Nina's arm and escorted her to the door.

Nina waited until they were outside before she turned on him crossly. 'You had no right to cancel my arrangements like that!'

He gave her a glowering look as he unlocked his car. 'Your arrangements were putting my niece at risk. Look at her. She has obviously been crying hysterically; she is feverish and over-tired.' He took the baby from her arms and cuddled her close, glaring over the top of her head at Nina. 'I cannot believe you would be so insensitive to leave a clearly distraught baby with total strangers.'

'Oh, for God's sake!' She let out a frustrated breath. 'Get into the real world, Marc. Mothers all over the world put their children into childcare. They need to in order to work.'

'But you do not work so it is not necessary for you to engage such services.' He turned away to secure Georgia in her baby seat in the car.

'How did you know I was here?' she asked after a moment of silence. 'Were you following me?'

He straightened from settling Georgia. 'In the light of that magazine article, I decided it was wise to keep some tabs on you.'

She gnawed at her bottom lip and then began uncertainly, 'Marc...' She tried not to be put off by his stern expression and continued, 'I haven't been completely truthful to you. I...I have a job.'

'What sort of job?'

'One that pays me money.'

'That certainly narrows it down a bit,' he commented dryly. 'What sort of work do you do?'

'I'm a librarian.'

She saw the flicker of surprise come and go in his dark gaze as it held hers. 'Andre did not mention it.'

'Andre didn't know. It's been a…recent thing. I wanted to improve myself…for Georgia's sake.'

'Doesn't one have to study at university in order to be a librarian?'

'Er…yes, I did that a few years ago…before I…you know…went off the rails a bit.'

Nina knew she was skating on ever thinning ice. She could see the suspicion growing in his eyes as he watched her.

'How important is this job to you?' he asked after a small pause.

She looked at the now sleeping baby in her baby seat in the back. 'Not as important as Georgia,' she answered softly.

Marc drew in a breath and opened the passenger door for her. 'Get in. We will talk about this later.'

Nina slipped into the seat and clipped on her belt, all the time wondering if she had blown it. She hoped not, for the thought of never seeing her niece again was unbearably painful.

She spent the rest of the silent journey wondering how she was going to maintain her charade. When she looked up she saw that they were not at her flat but in the driveway of an imposing looking mansion in the exclusive harbourside suburb of Mosman.

She turned in her seat to look at him. 'This is your house?'

He looked at her for so long without responding that she wondered if she had just made another slip. She'd always assumed that Nadia had met Andre in hotels but it suddenly occurred to her that perhaps she had visited him at home—this home.

'Do you not remember coming here?' he asked.

She disguised a nervous swallow. 'It looks vaguely familiar,' she hedged.

The line of his mouth thinned in anger. 'You appear to have

a very convenient memory pattern, Nina. You simply delete the things you find distasteful to recall.' He got out of the car and came around to open her door, his expression still tight with fury. 'Let me remind you, then. You came here the night before Andre was killed, banging on the door and making a general nuisance of yourself. God knows where you had left Georgia. My brother had no choice but to let you in and once inside you tried to seduce him.' His dark eyes glittered dangerously. 'Remember now?'

She opened and closed her mouth, not sure how to answer.

'I could go into more detail if you would like,' he added. 'Or are you starting to remember all by yourself?'

'I don't need you to tell me how dreadfully I behaved,' she said, lowering her gaze. 'I was…upset and lonely, and I didn't know which way to turn.'

Marc watched her in silence, wondering if he was being too harsh. There was so much about her that was confusing. Just when he thought he had her all figured out she would go and do something that would contradict his assessment of her. Lately he had even started to question all his brother had told him, wondering if Andre had deliberately painted a worse picture in order to exonerate himself from any wrongdoing on his part.

Having a baby without the support of the father was undoubtedly a stressful, worrying experience and, although her behaviour had been outrageous, a part of him wanted to find an excuse so that he didn't have to hate her quite so strenuously. It had only been just over four months since she'd given birth; she might even be suffering from some sort of hormonal imbalance and the last thing she needed was the heavy hand of judgement. It intrigued him that she could be so shallow one minute and yet so devoted to her daughter the next. Unless it was all an act for his benefit, he knew he would have a fight on his hands convincing any magistrate she wasn't a fit mother. The truth was, as far as he could tell so far, she was a wonderful mother. The very fact that she had tried to juggle work and childcare in order to provide for her daughter without a hand-out from him, even though he'd offered it, surely demonstrated that she was keen to turn her bad reputation around.

'It is pointless discussing it now,' he said. 'What is done is done and cannot be undone.'

As they approached the large front door of his house a woman in her late fifties and of Italian descent appeared in its frame. She greeted her employer with deference but the look she cast Nina's way would have curdled milk.

Marc spoke to her in Italian but, to Nina's surprise, he didn't say anything remotely derogatory about her. He simply informed the housekeeper of his plan to marry within the next few days and that Nina and Georgia were to be made as comfortable as possible.

The woman muttered something Nina didn't quite catch and Marc admonished her. 'Yes, Lucia, I do know what I am doing and why I am doing it. You will treat both Nina and Georgia with respect at all times.'

The housekeeper grunted something in reply and sidled away as Marc turned to Nina. 'Just as well you do not understand my language,' he said. 'You have not made a good impression, it seems.'

'No, I imagine not.'

She followed him inside and tried not to look too much in awe of her surroundings, but it was impossible at times not to openly gasp at the priceless works of art which hung from every wall and the plush furnishings that spoke of unlimited wealth.

'I will have Lucia bring us coffee shortly,' Marc informed her as he opened the double doors leading to a formal sitting room. 'But first I would like to speak to you about the arrangements I have made for our marriage.'

Nina followed him into the room, watching as he repositioned Georgia, who was still fast asleep in his arms. He indicated for her to be seated and once she had sunk to the sofa he too sat down, his long legs stretching out in front of him as he tucked Georgia close to his chest.

'I have to go to Hong Kong on business,' he said. 'I will be away until the day before our wedding.'

'I see.'

'I would like you to move in here while I am away to settle Georgia into her new home. Lucia can help you with Georgia so you can continue to work, if that is what you would like to do, although you will need to take some leave of absence, as the day after the wedding we will be leaving for a short trip to Sorrento in Italy to visit my father.'

Nina had to stop herself from springing off the sofa in agitation. She stared at him in shock and consternation. She couldn't leave the country with a child that wasn't hers! And, even if she dared to do so and wasn't stopped, how would she cope with a long-haul flight after what had happened the last time she'd flown? Her flight home from a friend's wedding in Auckland had hit severe turbulence during a storm. It had been the most frightening experience of her life and she had not flown since. The mere thought of boarding a plane made her break out in a sweat, but boarding it with a small child in tow could only be a hundred times worse.

'I—I can't go,' she said. 'I don't like flying.'

'Oh, really?' He gave her one of his cynical looks. 'Is this a recent thing?'

'Yes. I had a bad experience three years ago.'

'But I assume not bad enough to prevent you from flying to Paris last year to hound Andre,' he observed.

Nina had forgotten all about Nadia's trip to Paris.

'I… It comes and goes. The fear, I mean. Sometimes I'm fine, other times I get all panicky.'

'Well, perhaps flying in my private jet with my staff to wait on you will alleviate some of your fears,' he said coolly. 'I will need your and Georgia's passports to make the travel arrangements.'

'I would really prefer not to go.' She got to her feet and began to pace back and forth. 'I have to work.'

'I think in the interests of Georgia you might consider taking leave from work. Most new mothers take a few months off. I am providing you with a generous allowance, so unless you are in particular need of any mental stimulation your job provides, I would suggest taking a break.'

Nina wished she could tell him what to do with his money but unless she went along with Nadia's plan everything she had fought so hard for would be lost.

'What am I supposed to do with my time?' she asked after a moment or two of silence.

'Look after your child,' he answered. 'I do not expect you to do so all on your own, of course. I will help whenever I can and so too will Lucia. She is an experienced mother and grandmother and will do an exemplary job of minding Georgia whenever the need arises.'

'I don't want to live here until absolutely necessary.'

'You have no choice, Nina. I have already contacted your landlord and informed him you will be terminating your lease as of tomorrow.'

'You had no right to do that!'

'I have every right. I will be your husband in a matter of days. I would be failing in my duty to protect both you and Georgia if I did not ensure you were safely housed in my home as we begin our life together.'

'You're only doing it because you don't trust me, so don't insult me by pretending anything else,' she spat.

'You are correct. I do not trust you. As soon as my back is turned, no doubt you will be off with one of your men friends, but this way I get to keep Georgia safe.'

'You make it sound as if I mean to do her harm.'

He held her fiery gaze with equanimity. 'You may not intentionally mean to do so but your erratic, irresponsible behaviour of the past indicates you do not always act in her best interests.'

'It seems I have little choice in all of this. You have organised it all without consulting me.'

'All I have arranged was what we agreed on. We will live as man and wife and jointly raise Georgia until such time as we both feel the marriage is no longer viable.'

'It's not viable now! We hate the sight of each other; what sort of marriage is that going to be?'

There was a knock at the door and the housekeeper came in bearing a tray of coffee and biscotti. Marc exchanged a few words with her and she left with a black look cast in Nina's direction.

'Do not take any notice,' Marc said once the housekeeper had left. 'She had rather a soft spot for my brother.'

'So, like you, she blames me for his death?'

Marc gave her a studied look before responding. 'It is hard sometimes for those who are still grieving to see the other side of the story.' He glanced down at the sleeping infant in his arms and added, 'It cannot have been easy for you, left alone with a child to raise without her father's support.' He lifted his eyes to hers and asked, 'Did you ever consider an abortion?'

'I—I was talked out of it.'

'By whom?'

Nina looked at her hands in her lap. 'By someone who has done her best to support me through my difficult years.'

'A close friend?'

'More than a close friend,' she said. 'More like…a sister.'

There was a small silence.

'I am glad you did not get rid of her, Nina,' he said. 'Georgia is my last link with my brother. Thank you for having her. I know it cannot have been easy, but I cannot tell you how much it will mean to my father to hold Andre's child in his arms.'

Nina gave him a weak smile as she reached for her cup, her stomach fluttering nervously at the thought of how complicated her life had become. Within days she would be married to

Marc Marcello, living with him and jointly raising Georgia as their child.

For now her secret was safe—but how long was it going to be before he realised he had married the wrong woman?

CHAPTER EIGHT

NINA was glad Marc was absent when she and Georgia moved into his house. It was bad enough dealing with the surly housekeeper, who seemed intent on making Nina as unwelcome as possible. Her treatment of Georgia, however, was an entirely different story. Lucia cooed and smiled at the infant with great affection and looked for opportunities to spend time with her alone.

Nina resisted her attempts at first but after a while realised the older woman genuinely cared for Andre's child so she allowed her to watch her once or twice while she attended to unpacking their things into the bedroom and nursery Marc had assigned.

She had handed in her temporary leave notice at work the day after Marc had left and was surprised how much better she felt knowing Georgia would not have to suffer the fear of separation any longer. The baby seemed happier already and, while she kept telling herself she was probably imagining it, Nina couldn't help wondering if Georgia was intuitively aware that she was living in her loving uncle's house and under his protection. Having grown up without a father, Nina knew Georgia would be blessed indeed to have someone as strong and dependable as Marc to nurture her throughout her childhood. It made the sacrifice she was making a little more palatable; her tiny niece would never know the aching sadness of not having a reliable parent to lean on.

* * *

On an impulse she wasn't entirely sure she understood herself, the day before the ceremony Nina withdrew the last of her savings and bought herself a wedding gown and veil. Without a mother or father to help her prepare for the wedding she had dreamt about for most of her life, she decided that no one was going to stop her being a proper bride, even if the marriage itself was just a sham.

She stood twirling in front of the full-length mirror in the boutique's fitting room, the soft organza floating around her like a fluffy cloud while Georgia chortled delightedly in the pushchair beside her.

'So what do you think, Georgia?' she asked as she lowered the veil over her face. 'Do I look like a real bride?'

Georgia began to suck on one of her tiny fists, her black-as-raisins eyes bright with alertness as she peered at her aunt through the cloud of fabric.

'Peek-a-boo!' Nina crouched down and popped back the veil to expose her face to her niece, who began to chuckle again.

She felt a rush of love fill her at the happy sound and, leaning forward, pressed a soft kiss to the baby's downy head, her eyes misting over with sudden emotion.

'One day I hope you will marry a man for all the right reasons, Georgia, a man who will love you to the ends of the earth and back. The way every woman deserves to be loved.'

She straightened and, spreading her voluminous skirts around her, turned to face her reflection in the mirror. The magnolia creamy white of the gown made her eyes a bottomless grey and the tone of her skin like velvet smooth cream. She knew it was quite possibly as close to stunning as she was ever going to get.

Too bad it wouldn't be appreciated, she thought with a little sigh.

* * *

Nina was still settling Georgia for the night when she heard the sound of Marc's car returning, the low growl of the powerful engine as it pulled into the sweeping driveway making her stomach turn over in reaction.

In less than twenty-four hours she would be his wife. She would share his name and his life but not his bed.

She heard him enter the house and the sound of his tread on the marble staircase as he approached the nursery where she stood watching Georgia drift off to sleep.

Marc met her eyes in the soft light. 'Hello.'

'Hi.'

She stepped away from the cot so he could check on his niece but in the small space she felt the brush of his body against hers and her pulse instantly quickened. She stood to one side and watched as he gazed down at Georgia, his features softening as he listened to the snuffling sound of her breathing.

He looked tired, Nina thought. His eyes were slightly bloodshot as if he hadn't slept well for days and his jaw looked as if it hadn't been near a razor for over twenty-four hours. She longed to run her fingers over his face to feel the rough raspy growth through the soft sensitive pads of her fingertips. She wanted to press her lips to the line of his mouth, to make it soften in desire. She wanted to feel him reach for her and…

She jerked away from her wayward thoughts as he turned his head to look at her, his dark gaze tethering hers.

'Is something wrong?'

'No.'

'You look…flustered.'

'I'm not.'

'Have you settled in?'

'Yes.'

'I would like to talk to you about our trip to Italy,' he said, moving across to hold the door of the nursery open for her. 'I will meet you in my study in twenty minutes. I would like to shower and shave first.'

Nina moved past him and made her way downstairs, taking the portable baby monitor with her. Lucia had left for the day so she set a tray with coffee and some cake the housekeeper had baked and carried it through to Marc's study to wait for him.

He came in a short time later, his black hair glistening with dampness, his face cleanly shaven and his casual jeans and long-sleeved close-fitting black T-shirt making Nina's pulse start to race.

'How was your trip?' she asked, disguising her reaction to him by concentrating on the coffee tray.

He took the cup she had handed him, his eyes meeting hers. 'Am I to presume you are rehearsing your role as my wife by serving me coffee and asking me such solicitous questions?'

She turned away from the cynicism she could see in his eyes. 'You can presume what you like. I don't care how your stupid trip went. I was just being polite.'

'Do not exert yourself trying to be polite to me, Nina. It does not suit you.' He took a sip of his coffee but when he met her slightly wounded expression he instantly regretted his terse words. He put the cup down and came across to where she was standing and, taking one of her hands, slowly lifted it to his mouth and pressed a barely there kiss to her fingertips.

She stood transfixed, her heart thudding behind her breast as she held his mesmerizing gaze.

'Why did you do that?' she asked.

'I am not sure,' he answered somewhat gravely. 'To tell you the truth, Nina, I sometimes feel when I am with you that I am dealing with two different people.' He paused for a moment, his dark eyes boring into hers before he added musingly, 'I wonder which one I will be marrying tomorrow.'

Nina pulled her hand out of his and put some distance between them as she tried to stem her rising panic.

'I can't imagine what you mean by that. You make it sound as if I have some sort of multiple personality disorder.'

'My brother told me many things about you but I am at a loss for I do not see any evidence of those things that disturbed him the most.'

'Perhaps I've changed,' she said, deliberately avoiding his eyes. 'People do, you know. Having a child is a very life-changing event.'

'Undoubtedly, but I cannot help thinking there must be more to it than that.'

'W-what do you mean?' She gave him a wary glance, her hands twisting in knots in front of her.

Marc watched the play of emotions on her face, the shadow of worry in her eyes and the way her smooth forehead adopted that slightly anxious look that he found so incredibly engaging. He had spent the whole time he was away thinking about her, wondering what it would be like to sleep with her, to have her long blonde hair splayed over his chest, her slim limbs entwined with his, her body satiated by his. It was as if, knowing she was forbidden to him, his body had decided to crave her relentlessly. He could feel it now, the steady throb of desire pounding through his veins, making him hard just looking at her.

He wanted to hate her, needed to hate her in order to keep her at a distance, but in spite of all his efforts his hatred was slipping away to be replaced by something much more dangerous.

'I sometimes feel as if my brother was talking about someone else entirely. It just does not add up.'

Nina was at a loss to know what to say in response. She thought of chipping back with a Nadia-type retort but couldn't bring herself to do it.

'Have you nothing to say, Nina?' he asked after another long silence.

She lifted her gaze to his, deciding the only way out of this was a complete change of subject. 'You said you wanted to discuss our journey to Italy. When do we leave?'

'We will leave the day after the ceremony. I will get Lucia
to pack for you. She will accompany us to help with Georgia.'
He reached for his discarded cup and refilled it from the pot
before turning back to her. 'I should warn you that my father
will not welcome you with open arms. He is an ill man who is
still grieving. I will try to protect you from any unnecessary
unpleasantness but I cannot guarantee things will be easy.'

'I understand.'

'The ceremony will be conducted at ten a.m. tomorrow,' he
said. 'It will be a low-key affair as befits the circumstances.'

Marc watched as she made a movement towards the door
as if she couldn't wait to be rid of him. He considered calling
her back but thought better of it. It was asking for trouble to
spend too much time alone with her. He was already treading
a very fine line and it wasn't going to take too much to push
him over.

As the door closed softly behind her, he wondered if he was
more than halfway there already.

CHAPTER NINE

MARC stood at the foot of the stairs the next morning and watched as Nina came down dressed in full bridal regalia. She gave him a defiant look from beneath her veil as she traversed the last steps.

'You look very nice,' he said, giving her a wry look. 'Going somewhere special?'

She twitched her train out of his way as she moved past him. 'Nowhere special, I just felt like dressing up.'

She was certainly dressed up, Marc thought with an inward frown. She looked absolutely stunning, just as a real bride should look. Why had she done it?

Nina stood silently beside Marc half an hour later as the brief ceremony was performed.

'You may kiss the bride.'

Her eyes widened in alarm at the celebrant's words, her palms sticky with sudden nerves as Marc turned towards her, his hands reaching out to lift the gossamer of her veil from her face.

'I don't think—' Her hastily whispered protest was cut off by the descent of his firm mouth towards hers.

She closed her eyes and did her best not to respond to the feel of his lips moving over hers, but it was hard, if not impossible, to ignore the warmth of his mouth heating her in places she didn't want to be heated. She felt every nuance of his mouth, his firmness against her softness, the way his skin rasped hers as he moved to gain better access.

She could feel her mouth swelling beneath the insistent pressure of his, her tongue moving forward inside her mouth as if seeking the probing warmth of his.

She felt something begin to unfurl deep and low in her belly but before she could identify what it was he lifted his head to look down at her, his dark gaze inscrutable.

She swallowed and turned back to the celebrant, who was smiling at them with indulgent approval.

For better or worse she was now married to Marc Marcello.

The reception was little more than a brief lunch with some of Marc's colleagues at a private function centre and as soon as it was over Nina changed into one of her sister's outfits, a silky sheath of a dress which clung to her rather too lovingly. She stood in front of the mirror in the powder room and tried to adjust the fabric so it didn't reveal too much of her cleavage, all the while doing her best to ignore the nervous flicker of unease in her eyes.

She ran her tongue over her lips experimentally. Her mouth looked the same but it somehow felt different. Her lips felt highly sensitive now, as if the brush of Marc's mouth on hers had triggered something under her skin, making her want more of his touch. Recalling the way his kiss had felt, his warm sensual mouth and the looming threat of his tongue about to slip between her lips, still made her stomach tilt alarmingly. Even now she could imagine how it would feel to have the rough maleness of his tongue searching for hers to mate with, arrogantly, demandingly—devastatingly.

She remonstrated with herself for craving something she could never have. What was wrong with her? What quirk in her personality made her ache for his desire, his approval, for a smile of affection or even a kind word?

She had no right to desire such things, certainly since it had been her own deception that had brought about their marriage. What would he do if he ever found out?

Once she made her way back out to the last of the lingering guests Nina found herself being escorted to where Marc's car was waiting, Georgia already settled in her baby seat in the back.

He drove to his house in Mosman, seemingly content not to engage in conversation during any part of the journey.

Nina used the time to get her head around the fact she was now his wife. His legal wife, she reminded herself with another deep lurch of her stomach. In name only, though. The mental reassurance restored some order to her insides, but then she thought about his kiss and her belly did another somersault.

'I have given Lucia the rest of the day off,' Marc said as he pulled into his driveway. 'There is a meal already prepared for later.'

Nina had never felt less like eating in her life. The thought of being alone with him in the big house with only her tiny niece as chaperon unsettled her terribly.

'I think Georgia needs feeding and changing,' she said once they were at the front door.

Marc held the door open and she slipped past him, holding Georgia like a shield.

'I have a couple of calls to make,' he said. 'Let me know if you need a hand with anything. I will be in my study.'

She was halfway through feeding her niece a little while later when Marc came into the kitchen. She looked up to see he had changed out of his suit and was now dressed in casual trousers and a long-sleeved dark T-shirt which hugged his broad chest, highlighting his superb physical fitness.

Nina tore her eyes away to concentrate on Georgia.

'Would you like me to take over so you can change before dinner?' he asked.

'No, I'm almost done,' she said. 'She doesn't seem all that interested in this anyway.' She put the spoon down and got to her feet, reaching for a cloth to wipe up a spill.

'She looks tired,' Marc observed as Georgia began to rub at her eyes.

'Yes.' Nina twisted the cloth in her hands, lowering her gaze to avoid his studied look.

'Nina…'

She turned away and scrubbed at the bench once more. 'I think I'll give dinner a miss, if you don't mind.' She tossed the cloth in the sink and turned back to reach for Georgia in her baby chair.

Before she could unbuckle the clasp Marc's hand closed over hers and she had no choice but to meet his eyes.

She edged her hand out from under his and straightened to her full height but he still towered over her, his body far too close for her to breathe with any comfort.

'Even if you do not choose to eat I have things I wish to discuss with you,' he said.

'W-what sort of things?'

'Ground rules, that sort of thing. I do not want you under any misapprehensions as to our arrangement.'

'I can't imagine what you mean by that.'

'Can you not?'

'No.'

'Living in the same house will mean we will, by necessity, be sharing a certain level of intimacy. I would not want you to get the wrong idea.'

She elevated her chin and injected her tone with sarcasm. 'Who exactly are you reminding of the terms of our agreement—you or me?'

His eyes hardened a fraction and a tiny nerve began to leap at the side of his mouth as if he was fighting with himself to remain civil.

'From what my brother told me, it appears you do not always play by the rules. It would do you good to remind yourself of them just in case you are tempted to act outside the boundaries I have laid down.'

'While we're speaking of breaking the rules, I thought your kiss was a little inappropriate at the ceremony,' she put in crisply.

His dark eyes hardened as they held hers. 'There will be times when wc will be required to keep up appearances.'

'What do you mean?'

'We will have functions to attend occasionally and as my wife you will be expected to act in a certain way towards me.'

'You mean fawn over you?' She gave him a disgusted look.

'I would not have put it quite like that.'

'How would you put it?'

'All I am asking is for you to show some level of maturity when we are in the company of others. Apart from my house-keeper and of course my father, everyone else assumes this is a normal marriage.'

'I'll do my best but I'm not making any promises,' she said.

'Good. As long as we both know where we stand.'

He turned away and left the room, the door swinging shut behind him.

Nina looked down at her niece, who was staring up at her with dark eyes bright and round with interest.

'Men,' she said, scooping her up into her arms. 'Who can work them out?'

Georgia gave her a wide toothless smile.

'Maybe I should try that,' she mused as she cuddled Georgia close. 'It seems to work for you. You only have to look at him and he melts.'

She buried her face in the soft down of the baby's dark hair and sighed.

Once Georgia was asleep later that evening Nina had a shower and changed into one of her comfortable tracksuits. Her damp hair was scraped back in a high ponytail, her face free of make-up and her feet bare.

She was on her way down the stairs when the door of the large lounge opened and Marc stood in its frame, his eyes taking in her casual appearance in a sweeping glance.

'Dressing down for the evening?' he commented wryly.

'One gets so tired of haute couture.' She fabricated a bored yawn, 'Besides, lugging all that expensive material around sapped my energy.'

'You look about fifteen years old.'

'Would you like me to change?' she asked, giving him a direct look.

'No.' He stepped aside to let her in the room. 'You look fine. Great, in fact.'

'Thank you,' she said simply, clutching the small compliment to her gratefully, hoping he wouldn't see how much he had affected her.

'Would you like a drink?' he asked.

'Something soft,' she answered.

'No alcohol?'

'I don't drink.'

He gave her an assessing glance as he handed her a glass of sparkling mineral water. 'A reformed drinker?' he observed. 'How very commendable of you.'

Nina wished she had the courage to toss the contents of her glass into his arrogant face. However, given her sister's behaviour over the last few months, she knew that his opinion, although distasteful, was probably warranted. Nadia had come in far too many times in a state of heavy inebriation for her to be under any illusions about the truth of his comment.

'There are a lot of things I have changed in my life lately,' she said instead.

He took a leisurely sip of his drink before responding. 'Dare I hope Andre's death has made some sort of impact on you to bring about these changes?'

If only he knew how it had impacted on her!

'It would be an insensitive person indeed who wasn't in some way affected by the untimely death of another,' she answered.

'Do you miss him?'

Nina stared into the contents of her glass, wondering how Nadia would respond.

'I try not to think about it,' she said.

'No, of course not,' he said. 'If you thought about it you would have to take some responsibility for it, would you not?'

She kept her eyes down, unwilling to face the venom in his. 'I did not have anything to do with the death of your brother.'

She heard the sharp chink of his glass as he set it back down and stepped backwards instinctively as he came towards her, his eyes narrowed into dark slits of wrath.

'Do you think by saying that enough times it will change what you did?' he asked.

Nina wished she could tell him the truth. The words hovered on her tongue but every time she opened her mouth she thought of Georgia and swiftly closed it again.

'You have guilt written all over you,' he said. 'I can barely look at you without thinking of my brother's final agonising minutes trapped in that car while he bled to death.'

Nina felt sick.

Marc swung away to refill his glass and she took the chance to draw in a ragged breath, her hands twisting in front of her in anguish.

She knew he was still grieving and was entitled to feel the whole spectrum of human emotions, including anger, but it didn't help to have it directed solely at her. She didn't have the hardened exterior of her twin to deal with such heavy criticism. Each time he berated her she felt as if another part of her was dying.

She turned to leave the room.

'Where do you think you are going?' he demanded as he put his own drink aside.

She bit her lip and gestured to the door. 'I think it might be wise to leave you to brood on your own.'

He closed the distance between them in two strides, grasping her upper arms in his strong fingers, his eyes glittering with fury as they clashed with hers.

'You think you can get off that easily? I will not let you escape unscathed. I am going to do everything in my power to make you pay for the destruction you have brought to my family,' he snarled down at her, his fingers tightening cruelly.

Nina did her best to appear unfazed by his anger but beneath the fabric of her tracksuit pants she could already feel the betraying wobble of her legs.

'I hardly see how marriage to me is going to help your cause. Not unless you're going to lock me up in some tower and feed me nothing but bread and water,' she said with a flippancy she was far from feeling.

She felt the bruising strength of his hold as his eyes bored down into hers and, unable to withstand the hatred burning there, she dipped her gaze to the harsh line of his mouth, her tongue snaking out to nervously anoint her lips.

'Damn you!' he growled and hauled her roughly against him, his mouth crashing down on hers for the second time that day.

Nina's gasp of shock and surprise was silenced by the assault. She tried to use her hands to push against the hard wall of his chest but it was impossible to remove that punishing mouth from hers. She was imprisoned by his hold, his body rammed up to hers, imprinting its maleness on the soft feminine curves of her frame.

His kiss became arrogantly intimate, the full thrust of his tongue through the seam of her lips taking all the fight out of her. She felt her legs begin to buckle beneath her and the hands that had pushed him away began curling into the fabric of his T-shirt to keep her upright.

His tongue roved the interior of her mouth in a search and destroy mission that left her floundering in an unfamiliar sea of sensation. She felt the feathering of need run down her spine to render her legs useless, the solid press of his muscled thighs against hers reminding her of his indomitable strength and power.

Her breasts felt heavy and full where they were crushed

against him, her lower body on fire where his hard length probed her blatantly, unashamedly.

He deepened the kiss even further, the pressure of his mouth eliciting a response from her she had not intended giving. She reprimanded herself even as she brushed her tongue along the stabbing length of his: he was the enemy, he was danger—but it did no good. Her body was on automatic pilot and acting independently of her common sense.

Suddenly it was over. He stepped back from her so abruptly that she almost stumbled, her body not quite up to the task of standing without his solid support.

His dark eyes glittered dangerously as he wiped the back of his hand over his mouth in an action that intended to inflict shame and embarrassment.

Nina refused to give him the satisfaction of seeing how close to the mark he'd come. Instead, she schooled her features into contempt and, reaching for a tissue from her sleeve, lifted it to dab at the swollen tenderness of her bottom lip where her tongue had tasted blood.

She saw his eyes follow the movement of her hand and was surprised to see a dull flush slowly ride up over his cheeks.

'Forgive me,' he said heavily. 'I did not intend to go so far as to hurt you.'

She sent him a scathing look as she tucked the tissue away once more. 'How far did you intend to go, enough to double my allowance?'

His mouth hardened. 'I have no intention of handing you anything more than the sum we agreed on. I told you before— our marriage will not be consummated.'

'Fine by me,' she snapped. 'But I suggest you run that past your body for clearance first.' She gave his pelvis a pointed look before returning her eyes to his. 'Somehow I don't think it's quite got the message.'

His eyes locked on to hers, the air between them crackling with palpable tension.

'I would advise you, Nina, not to push me too far. You might not like the consequences.'

She lifted her chin defiantly. 'You'll have to try a little harder if you want to frighten me. Don't forget I'm well used to dealing with ruthless men.'

'I could ruin you,' he reminded her. 'One exclusive from me and even a city as large as this will not be big enough to hide your shame.'

Nina felt the pinpricks of fear at his chilling threat. If only she knew what her sister had been up to she might have been able to call his bluff. But she daredn't risk it, not with Georgia's welfare to consider.

'I hardly see what benefit it will be to you to assassinate the character of the woman you have just married,' she pointed out.

'I will not act on my threat unless your behaviour falls short of the mark.'

'How very gracious of you,' she taunted. 'But what about your behaviour? Does that, too, come under scrutiny?' She touched her fingertip to her bottom lip and gave an exaggerated wince.

'You have my word it will not happen again,' he said, dragging his eyes away from her full mouth. 'Not unless you ask me for it, of course.'

Nina's eyes widened in defiance. 'How absolutely typical! You can't control your impulses so you blame me for inciting them!'

'You were being extremely provocative.'

'Oh, yeah? Well, you were being a complete and utter barbarian!' she threw back. 'It's no wonder your brother had all the ladies after him. Unlike you, he at least had a certain level of finesse.'

She stalked past him towards the door, but before she could open it his hand came from over her shoulder and slammed against the door to keep it shut.

She could feel him behind her, the heat of his body seeping

into hers as surely as if he were touching her again. She kept her gaze fixed on the woodwork in front of her, unwilling for him to see the bright glitter of unshed angry tears in her eyes.

'Let me go, Marc. I want to check on Georgia.' To her dismay her voice sounded defeated, nothing like her usual defiant tone.

His hand left the door to touch her on the shoulder, the gentle but firm pressure turning her to face him.

He was so close she wasn't game enough to draw in a deep breath in case the expansion of her lungs brought her breasts into contact with his chest once more. She raised her eyes to his, doing her level best to control the tremble of her chin as she fought to bring her wayward emotions under control.

'Don't make me hate you any more than I already do,' she said, her voice not much more than a thin whisper of sound.

He held her gaze for so long that Nina felt as if he were seeing right through her flesh to who she was underneath.

To whom she *really* was.

To what she *really* felt.

Just as her composure was threatening to crack he dropped his hand from her shoulder and stepped away from her. She watched in silence as he turned to his discarded drink and, tipping back his head, downed the contents in one deep swallow.

Nina took an unsteady breath and eased herself off the flat plane of the door.

'Marc?'

He turned to look at her, his eyes unreadable as he removed a piece of paper from the pocket of his jeans and silently handed it to her.

She took it with nerveless fingers, unfolding the paper to find it was a bank receipt documenting that several thousand dollars had been deposited in her account that day.

Her allowance.

She stared at it for a long time without speaking, not even noticing when Marc left the room, shutting the door with a soft click behind him.

CHAPTER TEN

NINA had not long returned to her bedroom when she heard her mobile buzzing from inside her bag on the floor. She lifted it out and stiffened when she saw her sister's name flashing on the screen. Lowering her voice to a whisper, she cupped her mouth around the phone and answered it warily. 'Is that you?'

'Of course it's me,' Nadia trilled. 'How soon can you send me the money? I'm in a bit of bother with some bills.'

Nina clenched her teeth. 'What about your boyfriend? Isn't he turning out to be the dream ticket you thought he'd be?'

'Cut it with the sarcasm, Nina. We had an agreement, remember? If you don't follow through I will come and collect Georgia and begin the adoption process and you will never see her again. It's your choice. You can phone bank the money to me right now or you know what will happen. Don't forget, I only have to make one little phone call to that new husband of yours and your secret will be out.'

Nina knew she was caught in an impossible situation. It was too late for explanations to Marc about who she really was. How would he deal with the news of her deception so soon after tying himself to her in order to give Georgia her father's name?

'How did the wedding go, by the way?' Nadia asked with a hint of mockery. 'Was it everything you dreamed of?'

'You know it wasn't,' Nina bit out. 'I felt like a complete fraud the whole time.'

Nadia laughed. 'But not for wearing white, darling. You're one of the few brides entitled to wear virginal white. What a pity your husband doesn't fancy you. I bet I could get him into my bed if the tables were turned.'

Something in her sister's tone irked Nina enough to respond. 'Actually, he does fancy me.'

Nadia's mocking chuckle grated on Nina's nerves. 'Only because he thinks you're me. If you were acting in your own personality he wouldn't take a second look. You're too boring.'

Nina held on to her temper with an effort. 'I don't think it's such a good idea for you to call me. If someone other than me picks up my phone—'

'I'm going to keep calling you until the money is in my account,' Nadia threatened. 'And if I don't get you on this phone I'll try the land line.'

Nina let out a sigh of resignation. 'All right, I'll do it. I will transfer the money.'

'Atta girl,' Nadia cooed. 'I knew you'd see sense in the end. *Ciao!*'

Nina waited until her fingers had stopped shaking before pressing in the necessary digits to process the transaction. Once it was done she did her best to settle for the night but she found it impossible to relax enough to get to sleep. But, strangely enough, it wasn't the money and what she had just done with it that was keeping her awake. No matter how hard she tried, she couldn't get the feel of Marc's mouth out of her mind, the way his tongue had darted with male urgency into the soft recesses of her mouth, making a mockery of every single kiss she'd ever had bestowed upon her in the past.

Marc didn't kiss tentatively or even in an exploratory manner. He kissed with ferocious intent, setting her blood instantly alight. She could still feel the pounding of it as it ran through her veins, making her heart skip as if it just couldn't keep up with the pace of her pulse.

It was impossible to ignore her growing awareness of him,

the way he made her feel when he so much as looked at her with the dark censure of his eyes. She felt her skin rise in re-action every time, the soft hairs at the back of her neck stand-ing to attention as if waiting for his hand to reach out and touch her there.

She couldn't believe her own foolishness. She had fallen in love with a man who had nothing but hatred for her. Even if he found out the truth about who she really was, she knew he would never forgive her for deceiving him. How could he? She wasn't Georgia's mother. She could not give him what he wanted because what he wanted wasn't hers to give.

She gave the pillow another frustrated thump before flopping back down. This was hopeless. What she needed was exercise and plenty of it. She glanced at the bedside clock and grimaced when she saw it was well past midnight. Too late for a walk around the block. Then she thought about the gym and pool downstairs, and her legs were already over the side of the bed when she hesitated.

Could she risk it?

What if Marc heard her?

She rummaged for her faded bathing suit before she could change her mind. A long swim in the heated lap pool was just what she needed. It was a huge house, and besides, Marc was probably already deeply asleep.

She didn't bother with turning on the lights; instead she put the baby monitor remote on top of her towel on one of the com-fortable-looking loungers and slipped into the warm silvery moonlit water.

Her tense muscles began to unfurl as the water held her in its liquid embrace, the slip and slap of the water against the sides of the pool the only sound as she carved her way through length after length.

She stopped to re-tie her loosened hair and, blinking the water out of her eyes, looked up to see a pair of very male tanned legs standing on the pool deck. She slowly lifted her head and locked gazes with Marc.

He stood looking down at her for a long moment while the silence crawled around them.

'What's wrong, Nina?' he asked. 'Are you finding it difficult to get to sleep alone?'

She tilted her chin at him. 'No, are you?'

His eyes dipped to where the water was lapping against her breasts and she felt a shiver of reaction pass through her as if he had just brushed her there with his fingers. She felt her nipples begin to push against the worn Lycra of her bathing suit, the bare skin of her arms and legs prickling in awareness. She tried not to stare at his lean tanned body but it was incredibly difficult to ignore the flat plane of his stomach, the rippling muscles of his abdomen and the dark trail of hair that disappeared into his black shorts.

She craned her neck to maintain eye-contact, her stomach giving a little startled moth-like flutter when he began to lower himself into the water.

'W-what are you doing?' She shrank away.

'What do you think I am doing?' he asked.

She turned to get out but her foot slipped on the steps and she went under instead. She felt Marc's hands on her waist as he steadied her, his body so close behind her she could feel every ridge and plane as she came upright.

The air she desperately needed in order to take her next breath stopped somewhere in the middle of her throat as he slowly turned her around so she was facing him. She could feel the magnetic pull of his body, drawing her closer and closer, even as the rational part of her brain insisted she step out of his hold. His fingers spanning her waist tightened fractionally, and one of his hard muscled thighs came between her trembling ones.

'I don't think this is such a good idea,' she said, hoping he wouldn't notice the nervous up and down movement of her throat.

'What is not a good idea?' he asked, his eyes burning into hers.

'Th-think of what it could cost you…' Her eyes skittered away from his as she felt his hard thigh press even closer.

His hands slid upwards from her waist to hold her shoulders so he could secure her shifting gaze, his voice low and deep as if it had been dragged across gravel. 'Do you think I give a damn about the money?'

She moistened her lips and then wished she hadn't when his gaze dipped to her mouth and lingered there.

'It's a l-lot of money…and if it was doubled…' She stared at the line of his mouth, wondering if he was going to allow himself to kiss her. Just one kiss. That wouldn't be breaking his vow to keep the marriage unconsummated, would it?

His head came down slowly, his mouth stopping a mere breath away from the tingling surface of hers. Her eyelids fluttered closed as she felt herself rock towards him, her body seeking the hard warmth of his like a small iron filing did a too-powerful magnet.

At the first touch of his lips on hers heat licked like a hot tongue of flame, igniting her senses into a blazing roaring fire of need. He plundered her mouth, sending her head snapping back as his tongue thrust determinedly into her moist warmth, his arms pulling her into him where his body pulsed and throbbed.

Her hands went around his neck, her fingers plunging into the thickness of his hair, her breasts tight against his chest, their aching points nothing to the storm that had just erupted between her thighs. She could feel the dampness of need he'd awakened, the silk of sensual desire that called out for him with silent but fragrant pleas.

His hands came to her breasts, shaping them through the worn fabric, his warm palms covering her possessively, his mouth still determined on hers. He pushed the shoulder straps aside and uncovered her, the roughened edge of his fingertips running over her nipples until she ached to feel the rasp of his tongue there as well.

As if she had spoken her need out loud, he lifted his mouth off hers and bent his head to her exposed breasts, moving his mouth and tongue in tightening circles until she became unsteady on her feet.

He came back to her mouth, taking it with renewed pressure as if in tune with the fire of need he was fighting to control.

Her hands slipped down to his waist, her inexpert fingers skating over his shorts where they were distended, his erection reaching towards her, as if seeking her feathering touch.

He groaned into her mouth as she shaped him, and again, even more deeply, when her fingers slipped inside to where he pulsed with increasing urgency.

He tore his mouth off hers and stared down at her, his dark eyes burning with unrelieved need, his chest rising and falling against hers as he struggled to rein in his galloping breath.

'This is exactly what you planned, is it not?' he said through gritted teeth. 'You wanted to make me eat my words, every one of them.'

'No!' Her hands fell away from his body with a little splash. 'No, of course not.'

He gave a rough grunt of derision. 'It's another of your tricks. You like to play the innocent now and again to put me off the scent of your real motives.' He dropped his hold and stepped back from her, his eyes still scorching her with contempt.

'Marc…I—'

'I know what you are up to.' He launched himself out of the pool and turned around to glare down at her. 'You will not rest until you have me begging. That is what you want, isn't it, Nina? Your final triumph in the face of Andre's rejection would be to have his older brother on his knees, offering you anything you want in exchange for your body. That is why you did not ask for payment, isn't it? To make me think you were not after money when in fact you are after so much more.'

'But I'm not after—'

'Get out of my sight,' he barked at her. 'Take your lies and your deceptive little games out of my damn sight!'

Nina got out of the pool with quiet dignity, her sense of pride refusing to allow him to intimidate her with his fury. She could tell he was angrier with himself than with her. Angry that he wanted her in spite of all he'd said to the contrary. But she felt sure this wasn't just about the money, it was about pride—his pride.

'You can't order me about like that,' she said, standing in front of him. 'I won't allow you to.'

Something moved behind his eyes as he stepped towards her again. 'You will not *allow* me to?' he asked with a curl of his lip.

'No,' she said, holding his gaze. 'I won't allow you to speak to me in such a way.'

He drew himself up to his full height, his mouth tightening as he looked down at her. 'Tell me, Nina, how are you going to stop me?'

She moistened her lips, her stomach giving a tiny quiver at the fiery intensity of his gaze. 'I'll think of something.'

He threw his head back and laughed.

Nina pursed her lips and frowned at him. 'You have appalling manners. I suppose it comes from having so much money. You think you can get people to do what you want by writing a cheque or issuing autocratic demands.'

'Well, well, well,' he drawled. 'Look at the pretty little pot telling off the kettle for being black.'

'You know what your trouble is, Marc?' she said, incensed by his attitude. 'You don't like yourself. You keep blaming me for your brother's death but I get this distinct impression that you actually blame yourself. I might be a convenient scapegoat but I will not have you browbeat me to appease your own sense of inadequacy.'

It became instantly obvious to Nina that she'd hit him on a particularly raw nerve. She saw it in the sudden flare of anger in his black eyes and in the tight clench of his hands as he held them by his sides as if he didn't trust himself not to use them against her.

He didn't speak for a long time but his silence was more menacing than any blistering statement could be, she thought as she stood before him defiantly.

'Tell me something, Nina.' He tipped up her chin with one long determined finger. 'Tell me why you fell in love with my brother.'

She froze at his words, her eyes flaring in panic, her heart ramming against her ribcage as she did her best to hold his hard penetrating look.

'You did love him, did you not?' he asked when she didn't answer.

Nina lowered her gaze to concentrate on the beads of moisture still clinging to the strong column of his neck. She couldn't bring herself to tell him yet another lie.

'No,' she said softly. 'I didn't love him.'

Marc's dark eyes narrowed dangerously as her gaze came back to his. 'You callous bitch. You callous little money-hungry bitch.'

She closed her eyes to block out his fury.

'Look at me!' He grasped her arms roughly and gave her a little shake.

Her eyes sprang open in alarm, her stomach twisting with despair at the hatred shining in his.

'You destroyed his life!' His fingers bit into her arms. 'You hunted him down and destroyed him for what? *For what?*' he repeated bitterly.

'Marc, I need to tell you—' she began.

'I do not want to hear anything you have to say,' he snapped, cutting her off.

'Marc, please.' Her eyes misted over and her tone became pleading. 'You don't understand—'

'I understand all right. I understand that you were not happy that Andre left you stranded without money. That is why you twisted the knife by threatening to have Georgia adopted, was it not?' He gave her a disgusted look. 'You never had any intention of giving her up. You were just playing a game to get as much money as you could.'

'I have never wanted money from—'

'Do not lie to me!' he shouted. 'You have played this for all you are worth. Well, I will tell you something, Nina.' He lowered his voice but it was no less threatening. 'You can have your money. All of it. I will double your allowance as of tomorrow.'

She blinked up at him in confusion. 'But—'

'I have changed my mind about our marriage,' he said. 'I've decided we will no longer adhere to the rules I set down.'

'You can't mean that!'

He smiled a chilling smile. 'Why so worried, *cara?* You slept with my brother without loving him. Sleeping with me will not be beyond your capabilities, I'm sure.'

'I don't want to sleep with you!' She wrenched herself out of his hold and stood glaring at him, rubbing her arms where his fingers had been.

'I think we could more or less say I have paid dearly for the privilege,' he pointed out ruthlessly.

'I am not for sale,' she said. 'I don't care how much money you throw at my feet. I will not be bought.'

'You *have* been bought, Nina,' he said. 'You have already pocketed one instalment.'

'I don't want your money, Marc,' she insisted. 'I never wanted it.'

She could tell from his expression that he didn't believe her. His mouth was tight with cynicism and his eyes diamond-hard as they tethered hers.

'If you did not want it then why is it no longer in your account?' he asked.

Nina's eyes flared in anger. *'You checked?'*

He gave a single nod, his expression still unyielding.

'You had no right to do that!' Nina could feel the panic beating like an out of time drum in her chest. If Marc was watching her so closely it wouldn't take him long to find out the truth.

She'd only transferred the money less than an hour or two ago. What if he orchestrated a paper trail of her account to see where the money had been deposited?

'You keep saying you do not want money but what is it you *do* want, Nina?' Marc said, breaking the humming silence.

She couldn't answer. How could she tell him what she really wanted? She wanted him. She wanted him to make her feel alive as a woman. She wanted him to make her feel desirable, irresistible and precious. She wanted to feel him in the throes of uncontrollable passion for her, not for who she was pretending to be, but for her—Nina.

She held her breath as his hands ran down her arms to encircle her wrists.

'Is this what you really want, Nina?' he asked, tugging her up against him. 'Is this what you crave more than money, the thing that I too crave until I cannot think straight for my need of you?'

She moistened her lips with her tongue, her heart doing a fluttery dance in her chest when she saw the way his eyes glittered with purpose.

His head came down, the heat from his mouth storming its way into hers, lighting a fire within her that refused to be banked down. She felt it crawling up her legs to pool in between her thighs, the heavy pulse of her desire for him only fanning the flames even further.

His tongue circled hers sensuously, the thrust and stab movements inciting her responses in a way she had not thought possible. Her teeth nipped at his bottom lip, her tongue delved and her hands clung where they could to hold him to her. She heard him groan, a rough low growl of male primal need that made her feel incredibly feminine and vulnerable and yet strangely powerful at the same time.

She felt herself being carried along on a tide of need so strong she had no way of resisting even if she had wanted to. This scorching physical chemistry had been crackling between

them from the very first day and it seemed that, in spite of
Marc's determination to resist her, it was becoming clear he
was no longer able to do so. The evidence of his desire for her
was breathtakingly unmistakable; she could feel his hard male
body pressed tightly against her softer one, his mouth working its magic on hers until she was like warmed honey in his
arms.

She felt his hands at her bathing suit straps where they had
slipped from her shoulders, and then the rush of air as he pulled
the material from her like a sloughed skin. Her legs quivered
as she stepped out of the pool of wet fabric at her feet, her
mouth still locked with his, her heart thudding with the hectic
pace of her fevered blood as he pressed her to the nearest cush-
ioned lounger.

He came down on top of her heavily, his legs entrapping
hers, his solid weight a welcome burden. She began to claw at
his shorts but he shoved her hand away as he dealt with them
himself. She gave a breathless gasp of anticipation when she
felt him against her, the length and satin strength of him searching for the entry of her body with a desperation she could feel
echoing deep within her.

He drove forward with a deep guttural groan which
drowned out the sound of her bitten-off cry as he tore
through her tender untried flesh. She sucked in a breath and
tried not to cry out again as he thrust deeply, but her body
resented the intrusion and made it impossible for her to hold
back the sound of her discomfort. She gave one short sharp
cry, biting down on her lip as soon as it escaped, but it was
too late.

Marc stilled his movements and, easing his weight off her,
looked down at her, his frown almost closing the space between
his dark-as-night eyes.

Tears sprang to her eyes and her teeth sank even further into
her bottom lip.

'*Cristo,*' he groaned and rolled off her in one movement.

Nina closed her eyes, her limbs suddenly feeling cold without the warmth of his.

'Nina...I—'

'Please don't say anything.' She scrambled to her feet without looking at him and reached for her towel.

'I am assuming from your reaction that you had rather a difficult delivery with Georgia,' he said, his voice flat and unemotional.

She wound the towel around her body without looking his way.

'Nina?'

'I don't want to talk about it.'

'We have to talk, whether you like it or not. I need to know.'

'What do you need to know?' She turned on him. 'Do you want to hear how Georgia was born after fifteen hours of labour without her father present? How her father refused to acknowledge her existence? Is that what you want to know?'

Marc stared at her, all of his carefully rehearsed accusations fading away.

'You have no right to cast judgement,' she continued. 'Do you have any idea of what it's like to be pregnant and alone? Do you?'

He drew in a breath and let it out on a sigh. 'No, I do not. You are right. I have no right to judge.'

'Georgia needed a father and my...I mean *I* needed someone to help me bring her into the world, but your brother wasn't interested.'

'He had not planned on having a child with you.'

'So what?' she asked. 'Whatever the motive when a child is conceived, it's up to both of the parents to jointly see to its welfare. Besides, accidents can happen.' She gave him a pointed look and added, 'I didn't happen to see you put on a condom just now.'

'I did not...you know...' He let his words trail off, a dull flush riding over his cheeks.

She raised her brows. 'Surely you know better than that? Pre-ejaculatory fluid contains thousands of sperm. You might very well be in exactly the same position as your brother.'

'If I am, I am prepared to meet my responsibilities. If we have conceived a child I will not walk away.'

'Even though you loathe me and can barely stand to look at me?'

He met her gaze without flinching. 'I will put my personal feelings aside if need be.'

Nina felt her heart tighten painfully at his words. He was so unlike his brother, who'd had his fun and had walked away without a backward glance. She knew Marc would stand by his word, even if it cost him dearly. How she wished she could tell him the truth!

She turned away before he could see the longing in her eyes. 'I wouldn't lose any sleep over it. I have no plans to get pregnant.'

'If it were to happen…' He raked a hand through his hair as he considered the prospect. 'You will tell me?'

She met his eyes for a brief moment. 'I would owe you that at the very least.'

His eyes fell away from hers first. 'I will check on Georgia. You should go to bed; you look…exhausted.'

She opened her mouth to deny it but stopped as she realised it was true. 'Thank you,' she said softly and moved towards the door.

'Nina?'

His voice stopped her hand from turning the handle and she slowly turned around to face him. 'Yes?'

His eyes didn't quite meet hers. 'I am sorry.'

Her hand on the doorknob fell away. 'For what?'

He dragged his gaze up to hers with an effort. 'I wish I had known the truth about Georgia's birth.'

She gave him a rueful little grimace and reached for the doorknob again. 'I wish you had, too. You can't imagine how much.'

Marc opened his mouth to call her back but the door closed on her exit, locking him inside with his guilt.

CHAPTER ELEVEN

THE first thing Nina saw when she came down with Georgia the next morning was a personal cheque made out to her lying on the kitchen bench, which was exactly double the allowance he had deposited in the bank the day before.

She wasn't sure whether to be angry or hurt. Was he paying off the bet out of guilt or to insult her even more? She scrunched it up and threw it at the nearest wall only to hear a reproving hiss behind her. She turned to see Lucia looking at her with her usual contempt, her dark eyes going to the ball of paper lying against the wall before coming back to hers.

'Do you wish me to clean that up, *signora*?'

Nina unthinkingly responded in Italian. *'No. Mi scusi*. I will see to it.'

Lucia stared at her, her mouth opening and closing like a fish.

Nina gave her a rueful look. 'I should have told you earlier. I speak and understand Italian.'

'Signore Marcello did not tell me,' Lucia said, her eyes narrowing slightly.

'Signore Marcello doesn't know.'

The housekeeper's dark eyebrows shot upwards. 'You have not told him?'

She shook her head and a little sigh escaped from her lips. 'There's a lot I haven't told him.' She turned to look at Georgia, who was sucking noisily on her fist. 'So very much I haven't told him.'

Nina became conscious of Lucia's lengthy, studied look.

'Signore Marcello told me to tell you that he has some business to see to. He will be home in time for us all to leave for the airport together.'

She gave the woman a faltering smile. '*Grazie,* Lucia.'

'He will be a good husband,' Lucia said after another little pause. 'You must give him time. He is still grieving; he is not himself at all.'

Nina inwardly smiled at the irony of the housekeeper's statement. Marc wasn't the only one who wasn't himself!

'Georgia is such a beautiful baby,' Lucia said, gazing down at the child. 'She has brought joy to Signore Marcello's life.'

Unlike her fake mother, Nina couldn't help thinking as she reached to tickle her niece's tiny fingers. 'She's my world, aren't you, Georgia?' She kissed each little finger in turn.

'You are a wonderful mother,' Lucia said. 'No one could doubt it for a moment.'

Nina looked around in surprise. The housekeeper had been nothing but hostile towards her for days. What had happened to bring about this sudden change?

Lucia's gaze was so intent and watchful that Nina had trouble maintaining eye contact. She looked away guiltily, unable to rid herself of the feeling that Lucia was starting to put some pieces of a rather complicated puzzle together in her head.

'There was a phone call for you while you were in the shower,' Lucia said into the sudden silence.

'Oh?' Nina tensed.

'I did not want the sound of your mobile phone waking Georgia so I answered it.' The housekeeper paused for a single heartbeat and added, 'I hope you do not mind.'

'No.' Nina swallowed. 'No, of course I don't mind.' She forced her voice to remain calm. 'Who...who was it?'

'She did not say, but for a moment I thought it was you. It was uncanny, really. Her voice sounded so similar.'

'Did…she leave a message?' Nina asked, staring at Georgia's starfish hands with fierce intent.

'She said she would call back some other time.'

'*Grazie.*'

There was another small pause.

'Signore Marcello has instructed me to help you pack for your trip.'

'It's all right, Lucia. I can manage. I haven't got much to pack anyway.'

The housekeeper gave her one last thoughtful look before moving away to complete her tasks. 'If I can help you with anything, Signora Marcello, you have only to ask. It will be my pleasure, I assure you.'

'*Grazie,* Lucia.'

Nina waited until the housekeeper had left the room before she released her breath. She sighed as she looked down at the chortling baby, muttering in an undertone, 'I'm in over my head, Georgia, and drowning fast.'

Georgia gave her a toothless grin and stuck her fist back in her mouth.

Marc was well aware of Nina's reluctance to establish eye contact with him as they prepared to leave for the airport later that day. She spoke politely to Lucia and was openly affectionate to Georgia as she settled her into the car, but each time her gaze swung to him it just as quickly shifted away, her cheeks turning a delicate shade of pink.

He slanted his gaze her way as they drove to the airport, frowning when he saw her hands moving restlessly in her lap and her bottom lip being nibbled by her teeth as she stared anxiously, almost fixedly, in front of her.

The memory of the intimacy they had shared the night before gnawed at him constantly, the feel of her body against his, her soft mouth feeding off his, her flinching cries when he had gone too deep for her.

He had been so confident he would be able to resist her but in the end he had not stood a chance. Even though his brother had walked away from her, Marc knew he was not going to find doing so as easy as Andre had. In spite of everything he knew about her, he still couldn't get her out of his mind. His every waking thought was of her and only her; even his restless slumber was haunted by his out of control need for her.

For years he had actively avoided becoming emotionally entangled with anyone. He didn't like feeling so vulnerable. It made him uneasy that the power balance had subtly shifted, leaving him open to the sort of hurt he had sworn he would never expose himself to again.

He couldn't make her out. If she was truly the sort of woman his brother had described why was she avoiding his eyes all the time? Andre had described her as a wanton witch who would do anything for his money or his attention. But after last night he was totally confused. It didn't make sense. She'd supposedly had numerous affairs since the birth of Georgia; the papers had been full of her exploits. Yes, he had rushed things a bit, but she had not given him any indication she wasn't with him all the way. Unless someone had got their wires very crossed, the Nina Selbourne he was married to was nothing like the woman who had pursued and subsequently destroyed his brother. He was the first to admit that people could change, but the sort of change Nina had supposedly undergone defied all reasonable belief.

'I am assuming from your continued silence that you are not looking forward to the flight,' he said after another lengthy silence.

Nina unlocked her hands and, searching in the bag at her feet, silently handed him the cheque he'd left that morning, her eyes communicating her anger.

Marc looked down at the cheque for a moment. Was this a trick?

He met her resentful gaze. 'I apologised for what happened last night. This trip will become even more unpleasant than it needs to be if you do not accept my remorse.'

'It's not your remorse I won't accept,' she bit out. 'It's your money.'

'I fail to see what you are so angry about. It was a bet, fair and square. I lost it and have paid up accordingly—or perhaps you are regretting settling for such a small amount.' His lip curled slightly. 'Would you like me to treble it to soothe your ire?'

Nina swung her head away from his hateful cynicism, her eyes smarting with angry tears.

'Come now, Nina,' he chided her softly. 'You have been paid for your charms before. Andre told me how much you enjoyed receiving gifts of jewellery and the like for your favours. That is, after all, the universal currency of mistresses. There is no point playing the affronted victim; it is just not you.'

No, Nina thought with a deep pang inside. It certainly wasn't.

A short time later their luggage was checked in and their documentation dealt with efficiently. Nina stood by Marc's side, wondering when the axe of officialdom was going to fall. She'd 'forgotten' Georgia's birth certificate, and if anyone asked for additional papers she was not quite sure what she would do, but to her immense relief no one did. They were waved through as if they were a normal, happily married couple travelling with their small child.

Marc's private jet was nothing like the aircraft Nina had travelled on previously. She settled into the luxurious seat as Marc dealt with Georgia beside her, his staff politely offering assistance and ensuring everything was to their liking.

As the jet taxied along the runway she sat with her fingers curled into her palms, her stomach churning in fear as the roar of gunned engines sent her backwards in her seat as the aircraft lifted off. She squeezed her eyes shut, panic making her skin break out in tiny beads of perspiration.

She felt Marc's hand reach for one of hers, the warm grasp of his long fingers incredibly soothing. She opened her eyes and encountered his deep dark gaze. She gave him a sheepish look and then looked down at their joined hands.

'I know it's silly, but I just can't help it.'

'It is not silly,' he said, giving her fingers a tiny squeeze. 'Close your eyes and try to sleep. Before you know it we will be there.'

She closed her eyes and willed herself to sleep but, as exhausted as she was, it was impossible to ignore Marc sitting so close beside her. She could smell his aftershave and even the fresh fragrance of his newly laundered shirt, and every time he moved in his seat she felt the gentle brush of his muscled arm against hers.

She caught him watching her once or twice, the slightly frowning thoughtful look in his eyes unsettling her deeply. Did he already suspect she wasn't who she had said she was? After last night he must surely be suspicious. She'd seen the same suspicion in Lucia's eyes this morning, the way she had looked at her as if seeing her for the first time.

When they finally arrived at the airport in Naples they were met by a member of the Marcello staff who had a car waiting. As they drove to Sorrento, Nina could pick up bits of the exchange between the driver and Marc.

'How is my father, Guido?'

'He is fading, Signore Marcello. He is living for the moment he sees Andre's child.'

'Yes…' Nina heard Marc's deep sigh, his tone immeasurably sad. 'I know.'

The Villa Marcello was situated a short distance out of Sorrento on top of a cliff overlooking the Bay of Naples, the surrounding hills densely wooded where olives and vines grew lushly along with lemon and orange groves. The villa was not old but it was built in the classical style and beautifully maintained with terraced gardens and cobbled walkways.

Nina looked around in quiet awe. The view across the water was nothing short of breathtaking; in the distance she could make out the shape of the Isle of Capri and the gulf of Positano and the warm summer air was scented with lemons and the salty tang of the sea.

She held Georgia close as Marc led her by the elbow towards the front entrance where another member of staff was chatting animatedly with Lucia, who had gone on ahead.

Lucia moved inside as the small Italian woman she had been speaking to turned and bowed respectfully to her employer.

'*Buon giorno*, Signore Marcello. Your father is waiting for you in the *salon*.'

'*Grazie*, Paloma.'

Paloma's dark eyes slid in Nina's direction but, instead of the frosty reception Nina had been expecting and mentally preparing herself for, the little woman smiled warmly. 'You are very welcome, Signora Marcello. My English is not good but I will try to be of help to you.'

'You are very kind,' Nina responded. '*Grazie*.'

Marc led the way into the *palazzo*, their footsteps echoing on the marble floors. Yet another member of staff was waiting outside the door of the *salon* and opened it as they approached.

Nina stepped into the room two steps behind Marc, her eyes going immediately to the figure seated in a wheelchair next to a large sofa.

'Papa.' Marc bent over his father and kissed both of his cheeks in turn. 'It is good to see you.'

Vito Marcello's thin hands gripped the sides of his chair as Marc brought Nina forward. 'Papa, this is Nina and your grandchild, Georgia.'

Nina held out her hand but the old man ignored it as his gaze went to the baby perched on her hip. She saw the sheen of moisture in his eyes and the slight tremble of his chin as he reached out a gnarled hand towards Georgia.

Georgia gurgled and dimpled at him, her tiny hands reaching down to him.

Nina had to fight back her own tears at the sight. She lowered the child to his lap and stepped aside, surreptitiously hunting for a tissue. She caught Marc's penetrating gaze and looked away, pretending an interest in the view from the window.

'She is so like Andre...and your mother.' Vito spoke in Italian, his voice husky with feeling.

Nina turned and saw the way Marc's throat moved up and down as if swallowing the emotion his father's observation had evoked.

'Yes.'

'For once you have done the right thing, Marc,' his father went on in his own tongue. 'I know it is not what you want, to be tied to such a woman, but it will soon be over. I have already sought legal counsel. When the time comes you will have no trouble taking the child off her.'

Nina had to fight hard not to reveal her comprehension. She pretended an interest in the view, her spine stiffening with anger.

'Papa, there are things we need to discuss, but not now,' Marc said in a low tone, his gaze flicking to Nina standing rigidly by the window.

Vito's lip curled in derision. 'You think she understands a word of our conversation? Then you are a fool, Marc. Andre told me she is an uneducated empty-headed whore. Do not tell me you doubt it? What has she done to you, talked her way into your bed?'

When Nina turned back around she saw the way Marc's jaw tightened as a tinge of colour rose over his cheekbones but she had no other choice than to school her features into a blank mask when his eyes briefly sought hers.

'Do not forget what she has done!' Vito continued heatedly.

'I have not forgotten,' Marc said, turning back to reach for Georgia. 'It is time for Georgia's bedtime routine. We will leave you to rest before dinner.' He looked towards Nina once more and spoke in English. 'Come, Nina. We will need to settle Georgia and get changed for dinner.'

Nina gave Marc's father a small polite smile as she held out her hand to him. 'It was nice to meet you, Signore Marcello.'

For the second time that evening Vito Marcello ignored her hand.

'Papa?' Marc prompted with a frown down at his father.

Vito made some inaudible comment under his breath and briefly took Nina's hand. 'Thank you for agreeing to bring my granddaughter to see me. I have not much time. She is all we have left of Andre.'

Nina blinked back the moisture gathering at the back of her eyes. 'I am so sorry for what you have suffered.'

Vito pushed himself away in his chair, effectively dismissing her. 'You know nothing of my suffering. Nothing.'

Marc took her elbow and led her away, softly closing the *salon* door on their exit.

'I apologise for my father's rudeness,' he said as they moved towards the huge staircase leading to the upper floors. 'He is still grieving.' He hesitated for a moment before adding, 'I probably do not need to tell you that Andre was his favourite son.'

Nina came to a stop and looked up at him. 'It's all right, Marc. I do understand. This has been a terrible time for you all.'

He gave her a rare smile, tinged with sadness but, for all that, still a smile. 'I sometimes wonder what my mother would have made of you,' he mused.

'Your mother?'

He pointed to a portrait hanging on the mezzanine level a few feet away. 'My mother.'

Nina took the remaining steps to stand in front of a portrait of a beautiful dark-haired, porcelain-skinned petite woman, her soft brown eyes sparkling with exuberant life.

'She's very beautiful.'

'Yes…she was.'

The tone of his voice turned Nina's head around to look at him.

He held her gaze for a heartbeat before saying, 'My father has never forgiven me for leading her to her death.'

Nina made a tiny gasp but no words came out. He looked at her across the top of Georgia's downy head as she buried it into his broad chest, her tiny hands splayed across his shirt. 'I was late. We had arranged to meet but I was late. I called her to tell her to fill in the time until I got there.'

Nina felt her breath bank up in her chest. She could almost sense what was coming, the guilt and the blame that clung like lead weights to one's conscience—what could have been done differently if one had only known.

'She was across the street when she saw me. She waved and called out to me…a motor scooter clipped her as she stepped out.'

'Oh, Marc.'

'She didn't see the other car. Nor did I until it lifted her and tossed her like a rag doll towards me.' He turned back to the portrait and let out a ragged sigh. 'If I had been just a few seconds earlier…'

'No!' She clutched at his arm. 'No, you mustn't think that!'

He extricated himself from her hold, securing his niece against him as he continued up the stairs. 'You cannot change the past, Nina. You, of all people, should know that. We all do things on the spur of the moment that we regret later.'

Nina wished she had an answer at the ready but there was a ringing truth in what he had just said. Her own impulsive actions had already caused her incalculable regret. If only she had told him right from the first moment what was going on, maybe things would not be as they were now. He was a reasonable man, a good man, a man of sound moral principles. If she had only told him that very first day of her fears for Georgia's safety, of her worries about her sister's motives—surely he would not have taken Georgia out of her life without thinking of the impact it would have on her niece?

But it was too late now. She had taken a pathway that had led her to this—a lifetime of deception. She had no choice but to continue in it, the lies and deceit banking up behind her like a tide of inescapable debris that at some point would come pouring over her, weighing her down until she would surely be choked by the brackish filth of it.

'Marc?'

Marc turned to look down at her, his brother's child asleep in his arms. 'Nina, this is my father's last chance for peace. I know this is hard for you…'

'It is not hard for me,' she said, touching him gently on the arm. 'I owe this to the memory of your brother. In another life, in other circumstances, he might have gladly accepted Georgia as his own. The timing was wrong. You have taken on the role as her father. I am…her mother. It is up to us to make her life what it should be.'

'And you are happy with that for now?' he asked.

She looked at the infant cradled in the protective strength of his arms. 'I am happy with that.' A tiny sigh escaped from her lips as she raised her eyes back to his. 'For now.'

A small silence swirled around them for several moments. Nina couldn't tear her eyes away from the lingering pain reflected in his. Coming home had affected him deeply, the rush of memories no doubt reawakening the guilt he felt over his mother's death. Hadn't she experienced the very same pangs? Even though her mother had ultimately been responsible for her own death, Nina still felt as if in some way she had failed her. If only she had tried harder to get her into a clinic or had visited her more often, maybe the outcome would have been different.

'Come.' Marc's deep voice broke the silence. 'Lucia will be waiting to settle Georgia. My father does not like to be kept waiting.'

CHAPTER TWELVE

ONCE Georgia had been fed and bathed, Nina left her in Lucia's care and made her way to the room Paloma had prepared for her.

It was luxuriously furnished, the huge bed dominating the room with its array of brightly coloured pillows and cushions, the floor softly carpeted with priceless antique rugs. There was a large wardrobe and dressing table and two doors, one leading to an *en suite* bathroom, the other to another room which, Paloma had informed her earlier—exchanging a conspiratorial wink with the hovering Lucia as she did so—was Marc's suite.

Nina tore her eyes away from the firmly closed door and moved across the room to the bank of windows, looking out over the majestic slopes of Mount Vesuvius. A slight breeze disturbed the sheer curtains, carrying the scent of orange blossom and honeysuckle into the room.

There was the sound of a knock on the connecting door. She turned and issued the command to come in, her throat drying up when Marc stepped into the room. He was dressed formally, his dinner suit making him appear even taller and more commanding, the whiteness of his shirt highlighting the olive tan of his skin and the darkness of his eyes.

'My father likes to dress for dinner,' he explained. 'Do you have everything you need?'

'Yes.' She pointed to the dress Paloma had laid out earlier.

'I'm sorry, I won't be long. I wanted to make sure Georgia had settled first.'

'I will wait for you in my suite. Knock when you are ready to go down. It will take you a while to find your way around the villa.'

'Thank you.' She waited until he had closed the door behind him before she stepped out of her clothes, wishing she had time for a shower but deciding it wouldn't do to upset Marc's father by turning up late for dinner. She made do with a quick splash at the basin and a touch of subtle make-up, tying her hair up with a clip in a casually arranged knot that revealed the length of her neck. The dress she had packed was one of Nadia's and, while it was very close-fitting, it was elegantly simple, the candy-pink chiffon giving her skin a creamy glow.

She gave the connecting door a tentative knock and held her breath as she heard Marc's footsteps approach.

'Ready?' he asked, his eyes sweeping over her with unmasked approval.

She gave him a small nervous smile. 'Yes.'

The dining room was as sumptuously furnished as the rest of the villa. Crystal chandeliers hung from the high ceiling, and the walls were adorned with priceless works of art as well as several gilt-edged mirrors that made the room seem even larger. The long dining table was set at one end for three people, the best of glass and silverware laid out in elegant style, with a fragrant arrangement of roses as a centrepiece.

Vito Marcello was already seated at the end of the table, his dark brooding gaze boring into Nina as soon as she stepped into the room with Marc by her side.

'You are late, Marc,' he said in Italian, his tone reproving. 'Have you not yet taught your wife how to be punctual?'

Marc held out the chair for Nina as he met his father's scowling look. 'It was not Nina's fault that we are late,' he responded in his father's tongue. 'I had to make several calls. It was I who kept Nina waiting.'

Nina sat down and waited until Marc was seated opposite before sending him a grateful glance. He held her look for a long moment, a small shadow of puzzlement passing through his dark gaze as it rested on her.

Vito muttered something under his breath and reached for his wineglass and took a deep draught of the rich red wine. Nina saw Marc's eyes go to the glass in his father's hand and the almost empty carafe nearby, the small frown between his brows deepening.

'You have a very beautiful house, Signore Marcello,' she said to break the uncomfortable silence.

'It will be Georgia's one day,' Vito answered in English and beckoned to the hovering staff member to refill the carafe. 'That is unless Marc has a son. How about it, Marc?' He switched back to Italian and added insultingly, 'You could take up where Andre left off. I am sure your wife will not mind if you pay her enough. She has opened her legs for many others, why not you?'

Nina drew in a breath, her hands tightening in her lap in anger, her cheeks storming with colour.

'What is between Nina and me is between Nina and me and no other,' Marc said with implacable calm. 'I would prefer it, Papa, if you would refrain from insulting her in my presence. She is, after all, the mother of your only grandchild and surely deserves a modicum of respect.'

Vito's eyes flashed with fury. 'She is the reason your brother is dead! She must be made to pay.'

'How?' Marc asked evenly. 'By taunting her whenever you get the chance? By twisting the knife of guilt all the time like you do to me?'

Nina sat very still.

Vito's glass thumped on the table so heavily that the chandelier above their heads tinkled along with the rest of the glasses on the table. He glared back at his son, his cheeks almost puce and his lips white-tipped.

'It is true, is it not?' Marc continued in the same even tone. 'You have always blamed me for my mother's death because you do not want to face the truth of the role you played in it yourself.'

'You were late.' Vito's words were slurred. 'You killed her by being late!'

'No, Papa,' Marc insisted gently. 'You were the one who was late. Do you remember how I had to wait for you to turn up to sign the rest of the documents on the Milan deal? You had been drinking. I had to wait for you to sober up before you signed.'

Nina watched in anguish as the older man reached for his glass and downed the contents, his chin wobbling as if he was having trouble controlling his emotions.

'It is easy to blame someone else rather than face the pain of the truth,' Marc continued on the tail end of a sigh, his tone gentle. 'Perhaps we are both to blame. I should not have covered up your drinking for as long as I did, but I only did it to protect my mother. I would do differently now that I know the price we all had to pay for my silence.'

Vito pushed himself away from the table and gestured for the young man who had poured the drinks to wheel him from the room.

Marc got to his feet as a mark of respect as his father left. Nina stayed put, her throat raw with emotion at what Marc had had to deal with on top of his own grief.

Marc's eyes met hers across the width of the table. 'I am sorry you had to witness that.'

'It's all right.' She looked down at the table rather than hold his gaze. 'I understand...you have no idea how much.'

There was a stretching silence.

Nina hunted her brain for something to fill it but couldn't think of a thing to say. She was conscious of the weight of Marc's gaze, as if he was trying to solve some puzzle about her that had previously eluded him.

'How long have you spoken my language?' he asked, bringing her startled gaze back to his.

'I…I studied it at school and university.'

'And yet you did not think it necessary to inform me of this?'

'I had my reasons.'

'Yes,' he said with a hint of resentment. 'So you no doubt could hear what was being said about you to use against me later. Is there anything else you have neglected to tell me about yourself that I should know?'

Nina lowered her gaze. 'No.'

She heard him get to his feet, heard his approach, her breath halting when he took her chin between two fingers and turned her head to look at him.

'Why do I get the distinct impression you are lying to me, Nina?'

'I—I don't know,' she answered lamely.

He tilted her chin even further so her skittering gaze had nowhere else to go but lock with his probing one. 'You are an intriguing woman, *cara*,' he said softly, the pad of his thumb stroking along the curve of her bottom lip. 'I wonder what other secrets those grey eyes of yours are hiding from me.'

'Th-there are no secrets.' Her voice came out thinly. 'I don't have any secrets.'

His thumb moved back and forth until Nina couldn't think straight. Her lips were buzzing with the need to feel the hard pressure of his, her breasts already tightening in anticipation of his touch.

He drew her slowly but inexorably to her feet and brought her up close to his body, his hands at her waist, his thighs brushing hers as his head came down.

A soft sigh escaped from her lips into the warm cavern of his mouth as it captured hers, her whole body singing with delight at being in his arms once more. She felt the thrusting probe of his tongue and began to melt inside and out, her legs weakening as she clung to him unashamedly.

His hands slipped from her waist to her hips, bringing her even closer to his pulsing heat. She felt the hard ridge of his erection and stifled a gasp of pleasure when he moved against her.

Marc dragged his mouth off hers and stepped back from her, his eyes glittering with desire. 'I told myself I would not touch you. After last night…'

She was saved from having to respond by the staff coming in with their entrée. She resumed her seat, picked up her water glass and drank deeply, all the time doing her best to avoid Marc's dark watchful eyes.

She was relieved when the meal was finally over. They had eaten most of it in silence, only occasionally exchanging a comment or two over the various dishes that were brought out from time to time.

Marc got to his feet once the last of the plates were cleared and came around to Nina's chair to escort her from the table. She got unsteadily to her feet and took his proffered arm as he led her from the room, while the nerves in her stomach fluttered frantically.

He opened the door of her suite for her and looked down at her, his expression unfathomable. 'I would like you to think about our marriage becoming a real one.'

Nina stared back at him, her heart starting to gallop behind her breast.

'I want what is best for Georgia and, in spite of what my brother told me, I now believe that you do too. That is why I feel it would be best if we conduct ourselves in a normal manner so as to give her the best possible environment in which to grow up. It would not be good for her to be around parents who bicker and snipe at each other all the time.' He gave her a soft smile as he reached out to tuck a loose strand of her hair behind her ear. 'You are still jet-lagged. I will let you sleep in peace. For now.'

She didn't want to sleep in peace! She wanted to sleep with him, but how could she tell him that without revealing her true feelings?

'Go on, *cara,*' he said when she didn't move. 'I am trying to be a gentleman here but you are not making it easy for me.'

'I—I'm not?' She moistened her dry lips.

'No, you are not. I only have to look at you and I want to bury myself inside you. Go now while I still have the strength to resist you.'

Nina turned and went into her room with dragging steps, the door closing softly behind her.

She wasn't so sure she liked the thought of Marc being able to resist her, especially when she had no such strength where he was concerned. But then he wasn't in love with her, she reminded herself painfully. He hated her even though he desired her, but he had decided to put that hatred aside for Georgia's sake. How much more would he hate her if he ever found out who she really was?

CHAPTER THIRTEEN

NINA woke some time during the night with the familiar cramps that had plagued her on and off since puberty, the clawing fingers of pain tearing at her from the inside. She stifled a groan as she dragged herself from bed.

She made her way to the *en suite* bathroom and, after swallowing a couple of painkillers, sat on the edge of the bath, willing them to work before she made her way back to bed.

'Nina?' Marc's voice sounded from just outside the door. 'Are you all right?'

'I'm fine,' she answered.

'I thought I heard you groaning. Are you sick?'

'Not really.'

'Can I get you anything?'

She eased herself off the edge of the bath and opened the door. 'I'm fine. It's nothing I haven't had before.'

Marc frowned as realisation gradually dawned. 'You are having a period?'

'You're off the hook, Marc,' she said as she made to move past him. 'You're not going to be a father; aren't you pleased?'

He caught her wrist on the way past and turned her back to face him. 'You look pale. Are you sure you are all right?'

'Georgia is fast asleep, Marc. You don't have to pretend you are the least bit concerned for my welfare right now.'

'You are living under my family's roof and therefore under my protection,' he said. 'If you are sick you need to tell me.'

She pulled out of his hold. 'I am not sick! I just need to be left alone. Is that so much to ask?' She felt the blur of tears film her eyes and spun around for the door.

Marc caught the back of her over-sized nightwear and, like an elastic band, she bounced back towards him. He turned her around and looked into her streaming eyes, something deep inside him loosening as he saw the betraying wobble of her chin.

He brushed the pad of his thumb across her cheek where a tear was making a crystal pathway, the softness of her skin like velvet beneath his touch.

'You are crying,' he said, his tone sounding surprised.

'You don't say.' She gave a little choked sob and brushed at her eyes with her free hand.

'Why are you crying?'

She lifted her head to look at him. 'Do you have a law against it, Marc? Do I have to ask your permission before I have a good howl?'

'No…I was just asking.'

'I'm crying because I always cry when I have my period,' she sobbed. 'I can't help it. I get overly emotional and start blubbering over the stupidest things.' She blew her nose on the tissue he handed her from the box nearby and continued, 'I didn't mean to wake you. I'm sorry…but I…'

'Hey.' His hand cupped the back of her head and brought it into his chest, his fingers stroking through the silky strands of her hair in soft soothing strokes.

Nina buried her head into his warmth, her cheek pressed against the steady thump of his heart, her arms going around his waist before she could stop them.

'Shh,' he said softly. 'Don't cry.'

His kindness and gentleness only made it worse. Her guilt over all the lies she'd told him assailed her and she sobbed into his chest all the harder.

After a while Marc felt her settle against him, her crying bout over. He stood with her in the circle of his arms, his chin resting on the top of her head, his nostrils filling with the gardenia scent of her hair. He wished he could freeze time and stand here forever with her, holding her close to him, his body silently communicating the love he had been unable to stop himself feeling in spite of her past.

'I'm sorry.' She eased herself away from him and let her arms fall to her sides. 'I've made your shirt wet.'

He looked down at the damp patch and smiled. 'That's all right. I was just about to take it off anyway.'

Nina gave him a little embarrassed glance as her hand fluttered in the door's direction. 'I…I'd better go back to bed. It's late.'

'Nina.' He captured her fluttering hand and brought it up to his mouth, his lips brushing each of her fingertips as his eyes secured hers.

'Marc…I…' She swallowed as his lips closed over her little finger, the rasp of his tongue instantly curling her toes.

'Do not talk, Nina.'

'I don't think we—' She stopped when he pressed a finger to her mouth.

'No talking,' he insisted. 'I have changed my mind. I am taking you to bed, in my room.' He kept his finger on her lips as he continued, 'Not to have sex with you; that can wait. I just want to hold you.'

'W-why?' she asked as soon as his finger moved away from her mouth.

His eyes held hers for seemingly endless seconds before he answered. 'Because when I hold you I forget about my brother. I forget about my grief. I think of nothing except how you feel in my arms.'

She drew in a breath that got caught somewhere in the middle of her chest, her heart squeezing at the honesty in his dark gaze as it rested on her.

'All right.' She lowered her eyes. 'I will sleep with you.'

He led her out of the bathroom, his fingers curling loosely around hers as they walked down the passage to his bedroom, every step she took reminding Nina of every lie she'd told which had paved the pathway to this.

He thought she was Nadia and was attracted to the persona she'd projected, never once suspecting the woman he'd married was a fake, a total lying fake who had no business being in his life, let alone in his bed.

Marc pulled down the covers for her and she slipped between the cool sheets, carefully avoiding his eyes as she curled on her side.

She heard him in the *en suite* bathroom brushing his teeth and a few minutes later the sound of the shower running. She closed her eyes and willed herself to sleep before he joined her but her nerves were on high alert, finely tuned to pick up every single sound he made.

The bathroom door opened. She tightened her eyelids and, keeping herself to the furthest edge of the mattress, held her breath as he approached the bed.

She heard the soft rustle of cotton as he slid the covers back, felt the depression of the mattress as it took his weight and the sound of his small sigh of relief as his head finally met the pillow.

The silence seemed to be creeping towards her from every shadowed corner of the room, curling around her, making it impossible for her to relax enough to sleep. Her legs felt twitchy and uncomfortable and she longed to stretch the tension out of them but didn't want to encounter his long legs in doing so.

She squeezed her eyes shut and tried to count back from a thousand but she'd only got to nine hundred and twenty-seven when she heard Marc turn on the bedside lamp and felt him move towards her.

Her eyes sprang open to see him propped up on one elbow, his mouth tilted as he looked down at her. 'Are you always this restless in bed?' he asked.

'I'm not used to sleeping with—' She stopped mid-sentence as she realised what she'd just said, her cheeks heating from the inside out.

The smile went from his mouth. 'You mean that in the past you loved them and left them? Got the business done and moved on?'

'I wouldn't exactly put it like that.'

Marc wished he could control the tide of jealousy that assailed him every time he thought of her with his brother and God knew how many other men, but it ate at him regardless. He could just imagine how she had flitted from bed to bed on her hunt for the highest bidder. Hadn't his own experience with women taught him that in the past? Money was the biggest aphrodisiac for mercenary women and, although Nina was giving an Oscar-winning performance as a wide-eyed innocent, he had to remember it was an act, and it wasn't likely to last.

'How exactly would you put it?' he asked, unable to remove the contempt from his tone.

She moistened her lips and stared at the pulse beating in his neck rather than meet his eyes. 'I don't want to argue with you. I'm tired and it will only make things worse.'

'Did you ever spend a whole night with my brother or did you just service him and leave as quickly as you could?'

Nina flinched at his blunt crudity, her anger rising steadily within her. Her sister was promiscuous, yes, but she sure as hell wasn't a prostitute and she resented him implying it.

'That's a despicable thing to say,' she bit out.

'Did you ever spend a full night with him?' he asked again.

'It's none of your business.' She shut her eyes again and turned her back.

His hand came down on her shoulder and turned her over in one swift movement, his expression grimly determined as he held her gaze. 'Did he ever pay you for sex?'

'What do you think?' she said with a challenging edge to

her tone. 'You're the one who thinks he knows me better than Andre ever did. Do *you* think I would do something like that?'

Marc wanted to believe her incapable of such behaviour but everything his brother had said proclaimed her guilt. Besides, the allowance he had given her had disappeared almost as soon as it had been deposited.

After a tense moment that seemed like forever, he released her. He twisted round to snap off the bedside light and lay back down and closed his eyes, wishing he could wake up in the morning to find that the woman he had come to care for was someone else instead of the woman who had destroyed his brother's life.

'Marc?' Nina whispered in the darkness a few minutes later, but there was no answer except the deep even breathing indicating he had fallen asleep.

She flopped on her back and stared at the ceiling. If only she could fall asleep so easily, she thought with a touch of resentment. Her conscience was very likely to keep her awake for the rest of her life.

Some time during the early hours of the morning Nina became aware of strong arms holding her, the warmth of a large body behind her making her feel safe in a way she'd never felt before.

She moved one of her legs and felt the springy hair of Marc's legs where they lay entwined with hers. He mumbled something in his sleep and his hold tightened a fraction, one of his hands gently cupping her breast through her thin cotton nightshift.

She closed her eyes and tried to go back to sleep but it was impossible to ignore the heated probe of his growing arousal at her back. She felt it swelling against her, the heat coming off his body melting her like chocolate beneath a blowtorch. She felt her own body responding, the tightening of her breasts, the clench of her stomach muscles and the feathering feeling stirring between her thighs.

She drew in an unsteady breath as he began to nuzzle her neck, his mouth playing further havoc with her senses.

'Mmm,' he murmured against her skin, the movement of his mouth tickling her. 'You taste wonderful.'

'I—I do?' She gave a tiny shiver as his tongue unfolded in her ear.

'Mmm.' His mouth moved towards hers, hovering just above, the movement of air when he spoke caressing her lips. *'Delizioso.'*

She shut her eyes as he closed the distance, the soft press of his mouth on hers sending her back into the mattress with a deep sigh of pleasure. It was unlike all of his previous kisses in that it was slow and drugging, no hint of urgency, although no less tantalizing. She felt the slow melt of her bones in his loose embrace, the way her spine softened where it lay against the mattress, her legs gently tethered by the length and strength of his.

His kiss deepened with the soft stroke of his tongue, the sensuous movement sending shooting arrows of need to her core. She could feel her body clamouring for more, his pace two steps behind her need of him. She groaned against his mouth as he sent a hand to the soft swell of her hip, the splay of his fingers drawing her inexorably closer to where his erection pulsed with thick, passion-charged blood.

'I want you so badly,' he said against her mouth. 'I do not think I have ever wanted someone so much.'

She sucked in a breath as he lifted the hem of her nightshift, the slow glide of his hand up the length of her thigh instantly reminding her of why she was in his bed in the first place.

'I can't.' She captured his hand to stall him, an apology in her eyes as she met his. 'My period, remember?'

He looked at her for a long moment, his eyes so dark she felt herself drowning in their midnight depths.

'I did not have you picked as coy about such things,' he said at last. 'It is terribly old-fashioned to be so squeamish about a perfectly normal bodily function.'

'I know. I'm sorry.'

'You have been doing a lot of apologising just lately.' He gave her a wry smile. 'Is there anything else you need to get off your chest while you are at it?'

Nina's eyes skittered away from his, her cheeks instantly growing warm. 'No! No, of course not.'

'Just asking.' He brushed a strand of hair away from her mouth with a gentle touch which brought her troubled gaze back to his as he'd intended. 'Sometimes, Nina, I think you are holding something back from me. Something important.'

He watched her throat move up and down in a small swallow, the nervous shadow moving behind her grey eyes another indication of her increasing uneasiness around him.

'What could I possibly be hiding?'

'I don't know.' He watched the play of emotions flitting across her face. 'I have been trying to work out who the real Nina is but I keep drawing a blank.'

'I find it hard to be myself around you,' she said, absently plucking at the sheet with her fingers.

'Why?' he asked. 'Because of my brother?'

No, because of my sister, she wanted to say, but couldn't.

'You've been so angry at me all the time,' she said instead. 'I'm not used to dealing with such a barrage of negative emotion.'

She heard him release a heavy sigh. 'You are right. Andre's death on the top of my mother's knocked me sideways. I have not been myself for ages; sometimes I wonder if I ever will be again. But I meant what I said about a truce for Georgia's sake.'

She lifted her eyes to his, her expression soft with empathy. 'I do understand, you know.'

He gave her a twisted smile. 'Yes, I suppose you do. You lost him as well and, even though you say you did not love him, when all is said and done he was still the father of Georgia, and that must count for something, surely.'

'It counts for a lot,' she said softly.

Marc settled himself back down with another deep sigh.

'Better get some sleep, Nina,' he said with his eyes closed.

Nina watched him for a long moment. The normally harsh lines of his face were more relaxed than she had ever seen before. She wanted to reach out with her fingers and trace over his aristocratic eyebrows, feel the ridge of his nose where it looked as if it had been broken some time in the past. She wanted to press her lips to the line of his, feel the way his mouth responded to her, fought with her, mated with her.

'Marc?' She whispered his name in the silence.

'Mmm?'

'I want you to know that I think you're a wonderful substitute father for Georgia.'

She felt him reach for her hand, his long fingers squeezing hers momentarily. 'Thank you,' he said. 'I love her as if she were my own.'

'So do—' She stopped, her heart giving a hard ram against her ribcage at the slip of her tongue.

She waited in agonising silence for him to pick her up on it, her stomach rolling in panic, her heart racing until she could feel the blood thrumming in her ears. But his breathing had evened out, his chest rising and falling at neat intervals, indicating he was already asleep.

Nina eased herself back down beside him, her breathing gradually returning to normal as she realised that so far her secret was still safe.

But it had been close.

Far, far too close.

CHAPTER FOURTEEN

NINA woke the next morning to find Marc lying propped up on one elbow, silently watching her. She felt warm colour instantly flood her cheeks and wished she had the aplomb of her sister so that she could wake up next to a full-blooded man without blushing to the roots of her hair.

She made a move to leave the bed but his hand came down over hers and stalled her.

'No, don't run away. Lucia is caring for Georgia. You are entitled to a morning or two off. How are you feeling?'

She shifted her gaze. 'I'm fine. The cramps have gone.'

'Good.' She heard him get out of bed but didn't chance a glance his way, not sure she could cope with seeing his body without the shield of his clothes. 'I have plans for you.'

'Plans?' She met his eyes briefly.

He shrugged himself into a bathrobe. 'This is your first visit to Sorrento, is it not? I think it would be nice if we left Lucia with Georgia this morning while I show you around a bit. We can visit the church of San Francesco and have lunch at one of the restaurants in the centre of Sorrento at Piazza Tasso. Tomorrow we can explore the ruins of Pompeii and then drive to Positano for a late lunch.'

'Are you sure Georgia will be—'

'She will be fine,' he reassured her. 'My father will want to spend time with her, under Lucia's supervision, of course. In the light of what occurred last night, I think it is best if both of us are not there.'

Nina was inclined to agree but didn't voice it. She was still feeling terribly unsettled by the exchange between Marc and his father. Vito Marcello was undoubtedly an ill man and his drinking of obvious concern to Marc, but when she considered the back to back grief he had experienced so recently she could hardly hold it against him.

'If there's anything I can do…' she offered, lowering her gaze once more.

It seemed a long time before he responded. 'Just be yourself, Nina. You cannot do any more than that.'

His words were like a dagger to her heart. If only she could be herself!

The morning was sunny and clear, the cobbled streets filled with avid tourists intent on seeing this exquisite part of the Amalfi Coast. The view from the public gardens above the typical Italian square of Piazzo Tasso was spectacular and Nina couldn't help feeling as if all of her worries and fears were gradually disappearing on the light breeze that gently stirred her loose hair whenever she faced the sea.

Being in Marc's company was like a potent drug; the more she had, the more she wanted. She drank his presence in, filling her senses with everything she most loved about him: his tall commanding figure, his darker than night eyes that now held no trace of their previous hardness, the softer line of his mouth now that a smile had replaced its earlier line of contempt and the way his hand reached for hers, his long tanned fingers threading through hers as if he never wanted to let her go.

He walked beside her, his broad shoulder against hers as he pointed out various sites of interest, his deep voice stroking over her like a soft caress. 'According to legend, it was here at Sorrento that Ulysses heard the tempting song of the Sirens, the nymphs who tried to entice passing sailors.'

156   BOUGHT FOR THE MARRIAGE BED

Nina looked out at the sparkling water, shielding her eyes from the bright sunlight as she tried to concentrate on what he was telling her instead of the way his lips moved when he spoke and how her stomach fluttered like a handful of butterflies every time he looked at her.

'It's so beautiful,' she said and, after a short pause, turned to look up at him. 'You must miss it terribly now that you live in Sydney.'

Marc's eyes left hers to gaze out over the water. 'Yes, but after my mother died I felt it necessary to get away.' He gave a small sigh and turned back to look down at her, leaning his back against the terrace railing. 'My father had decided Andre should set up the Sydney branch but it became clear after a while that he was not doing a good job of it.'

Nina held her breath, wondering if he was going to break his promise of a truce and blame her sister—and thereby her—for distracting Andre from his work, but to her surprise he didn't.

'Andre was a party animal, not a merchant banker, but my father refused to admit it. He resented the fact that I could handle business better than his favourite son,' he went on. 'But I think, given enough time, my over-indulged brother would have ended up very much like my father is now—a bitter, broken man with the crutch of alcohol doing a very poor job of keeping him going.'

She put her hand on his, her fingers curling around his, her expression empathetic as she held his gaze. 'Marc, I know you won't believe this, but I know what it is like to be the unfavoured child. It hurts so deeply to think that no matter how hard you try you can never quite please the one you love the most.'

Something briefly flickered in Marc's eyes and a small frown appeared on his forehead. He looked at her very intently and said, 'I thought you were an only child.'

Nina froze.

'How can you know what it is to be the unfavoured child when you are the *only* child?' he asked when she didn't respond.

The silence seemed endless as she hunted frantically for something to say.

'I—I meant I can imagine what it must be like…you don't have to have personal experience of something to understand what it is like—might be to feel that way…' Her fractured sentence trailed helplessly away.

It was only a second or two at the most before he responded, but to Nina it felt as if a century had passed.

'We should get back,' he said, pushing off the railing and taking her arm. 'The sun is starting to burn your face. I should have thought to tell you to bring a hat.'

Nina walked on unsteady legs as he led the way back to the car, her heart-rate all over the place at how close she had been to giving the game away.

The next few days passed in the same manner. Each morning Nina woke with Marc's arms around her, his body warm and protective, although he did not touch her intimately, even though her body ached for his possession. After breakfast he would take her out for the morning while Lucia cared for Georgia so Vito could spend time with her in his favourite private garden on one of the many terraces.

Nina was fascinated by the site of Pompeii. The crumbling buildings with their tragic history, the ancient relics, including bodies frozen in time by volcanic ash, chilled her blood as she stood silently looking at them, wondering how the people must have felt trying to escape the fury of Mount Vesuvius.

'It's just so sad,' she said when they came back out to the sunshine. 'To think that they had no time to escape, nowhere to run and hide, no hope of protecting their loved ones…'

Marc looked down at her troubled expression as she gazed out over the vista of ancient ruins. It was hard at times like this

to imagine her as anything other than a thoughtful caring young
woman with a soft heart for those who suffered. Where was the
selfish little whore now? he wondered.

During the first few evenings Vito Marcello ate alone in his
suite, sending word down, usually at the last minute, that he
did not wish to join them, but on the fourth evening when Nina
came downstairs a short time after Marc she found both Marc
and his father waiting for her in the dining room.

At first the meal was a somewhat stilted affair but it became
apparent to Nina that Vito Marcello was doing his best to make
up for his rudeness on the first evening she'd arrived at the villa.
He also seemed to be making an effort not to drink to excess.

'Georgia is a beautiful child,' he said at one point. 'I have
enjoyed my time with her each morning. Thank you for allowing me the privilege of getting to know her.'

'I'm glad you have enjoyed her, Signore Marcello,' Nina
said softly. 'She is very special.'

He gave her a lengthy look and added, 'Lucia has told me
what a good mother you are. And, since my son has informed
me you speak our language, I must beg your forgiveness for
speaking of you so insultingly the other night.'

'It doesn't matter. I've forgotten all about it.'

He cleared his throat and continued. 'I must also apologise
for the letter I sent you. Some of the things I said were…un-
forgivable. I am surprised you still agreed to marry Marc when
you had such a weapon to use against us.'

Nina sat very still. Nadia had briefly mentioned a letter
from Andre's father but she hadn't shown her the contents. Was
Vito right? Had there been a way out of marrying Marc that
her sister had deliberately kept hidden from her?

She felt Marc's suddenly intent gaze and turned back to his
father. 'We all do and say things on the spur of the moment.'

'You are very gracious,' Vito said. 'I had not thought you

capable of it. I am afraid Andre did not paint a pretty picture of your personality.'

Nina found it almost impossible to hold the older man's gaze. Lying to an old man, a dying one at that, seemed to her to be morally reprehensible no matter how altruistic the motivation behind it. She looked down at her plate, wondering how on earth she was going to get through the rest of the meal, when there was a knock at the door and one of the staff members came in at Vito's command and politely informed Nina that there was a telephone call for her.

She felt the full weight of Marc's gaze as she rose from the table, her legs threatening to give way beneath her as she made her way to the nearest telephone extension in the library down the hall. She closed the door behind her and, taking a deep breath, picked up the phone and held it to her ear. 'Hello?'

'Nina, it's me, your alter ego,' Nadia said with a giggle.

Nina's hand tightened on the receiver. 'How did you get this number? I told you not to call me! It's dangerous.'

'Surely I can call my own sister,' Nadia said sulkily. 'My married-to-a-billionaire sister,' she added with a suggestive drawl.

'You planned this, didn't you? You purposely didn't show me that letter.' Nina asked. 'You let me think I had no choice but to do as Marc and his father said, not telling me I had an escape route all the time.'

Nadia gave an amused chuckle. 'You fell for it so easily. Now who is the smarter twin? You think you're so clever with your university degree and gift with languages but you couldn't even get out of the Marcellos' plan for revenge.'

'What do you want?' Nina snapped. 'I've transferred the money into your account. Don't tell me you've already spent it.'

'I have, actually,' Nadia replied. 'That's why I'm calling you. I want more.'

'More?' Nina choked on the word.

'You heard me, Nina. I want regular instalments, starting tomorrow.'

'But I don't have—'

'Ask your husband to up your allowance.' Nadia cut her off. 'I want you to give me the bulk of it. That's only fair, don't you think? You have my baby so I should have your allowance.'

'I can't believe I'm hearing this. What's happened to Bryce Falkirk and your big film career?'

'Like most of the men I've been involved with, he's shown his true colours and left me high and dry,' Nadia said. 'That is why I'm relying on you to turn my life around.'

'Surely that is up to you?'

'One phone call, Nina,' Nadia reminded her coldly. 'That's all it will take. Or maybe I will pay your husband a visit. That would be even more effective, wouldn't you agree?'

'You wouldn't dare,' Nina said through gritted teeth.

'Oh, wouldn't I?' Nadia goaded.

'He would take Georgia off me without a moment's hesitation,' Nina said. 'She would be devastated; she thinks I'm her mother now.'

'Do you think I care what happens to that kid? This is about money, Nina. Just do what you are told and your little secret will be safe. *Ciao* for now.'

Nina replaced the receiver and made her way back to the dining room with a sinking heart. She knew she had no choice but to tell Marc the truth before her sister got there first, but she couldn't imagine how she should go about it. How could she frame the words in any way that would not incite his bitter anger? He had every right to be furious at what she had done.

Marc rose from the table as she approached. 'Is everything all right, Nina? You look as if you have heard bad news.'

'No...nothing important.' She forced her stiff lips into a smile that encompassed both Marc and his father. 'I'm sorry for interrupting dinner.'

'Not at all,' Vito said, gesturing to the staff member nearby. 'I am retiring early anyway. I am very tired. *Buonanotte*.'

Marc waited until his father had left before reaching for her hand across the table, his eyes holding hers. 'Do you know what I think we should do, *cara*?'

'N-no…what should we do?'

He gave a slow smile and rose from the table, pulling her with him. 'I think we should do the same as my father and re-tire early. While you were on the phone Lucia assured me Georgia is still sleeping peacefully so we have the rest of the night to be together. It is time to commence our marriage in the proper sense of the word.'

'Marc…I…' She stopped mid-sentence. One night in his arms, and then she would tell him. Surely that wasn't too much to ask? She would spend the rest of her life regretting it if she didn't have him make love to her properly just this once.

'I will not hurt you this time,' he said, stroking a finger over her anxious brow.

She stepped closer, loving the feel of his arms going around her, trusting him with all her heart. 'I know.'

He led her upstairs, his arm around her waist as they made their way to his suite, her heart picking up its pace when he closed and locked the door once they were inside.

He brushed his mouth with hers, once, twice, three times. His hands skated over her, his touch light but warm as he gen-tly removed her clothes while she fumblingly did the same to his.

He pulled back the covers of the bed and sat down, tugging her down beside him, turning her so that she was beneath him as he pressed her backwards with a heated kiss. Her body re-sponded hotly with each tantalizing thrust of his tongue, re-minding her of the intimacy of the union she craved. He moved his mouth from hers and caressed each of her breasts in turn, the warm moistness of his mouth stirring her into a mindless frenzy of need.

She drew in a breath as his fingers splayed over her intimately, the possessive touch thrilling her even as it terrified her.

He inserted one finger, slowly but surely, waiting until her body accepted him before going further. She writhed under his caress, her limbs becoming boneless when he explored her shape and form. She felt the tingling of her flesh as his fingers played with her, the tightening of nerves that threatened to explode with feeling.

'Relax for me, Nina,' Marc said softly. 'Let go.'

Nina closed her eyes and let herself fly with the feelings he had evoked, her mind going completely blank as wave after wave surged through and over her. She vaguely registered the gasping cries of someone and then, with a shock of sharp awareness, realised they had sprung from her own mouth. She floated back down, her body feeling as if it had been melted into a sun-warmed flow of golden honey.

Marc waited until she was totally relaxed before he moved over her carefully, his weight supported by his arms so as not to crush her.

Nina looked up at him wonderingly, her eyes wide and luminous as he eased himself into her with such gentleness she felt like crying.

'Are you all right?' he asked, stalling for a moment.

She wrapped her arms around him and drew him closer, relishing the feel of his satin strength stretching her.

'I'm fine…you feel so…so…right.'

He fought for control as her body gripped him, her words so in tune with what he was feeling it was uncanny. He'd made love many times, perhaps not as often as his less particular brother, but enough times to know when the chemistry was right. But with Nina it was more than just right—it felt perfect.

He bit down on his tongue when she moved beneath him, her small body fitting so snugly he thought he was going to go over the edge before he could stop himself. He felt the ripples of her muscles along him, the silk of her warmth caressing him as she held him close. He plunged deeper, muttering a silent curse under his breath in case he'd hurt her, but she simply sighed with pleasure, her head going back, her eyes dreamy.

He kissed her again, relishing the feel of her soft mouth submitting to the invasion of his tongue, the shy darts of her own making him swell even further.

In spite of her inexperience Nina could feel the struggle Marc was having. She could sense it in the way he held back from her, as if he was unused to letting go completely. She wanted him to let go, she wanted him to groan her name as he filled her, she wanted to soar with him.

She kissed him fervently, her fingers burying in his thick hair, her legs moving apart even further to make him go deeper.

He groaned as his thrusts increased their pace and depth, the muscles of his back tightening when her hands moved over them. She wriggled beneath him, her body instinctively seeking the intimate abrasion of his.

She sucked in a breath when his hand came down to touch her, his fingers seeking the pulse of her body with heart-stopping accuracy.

Now it was she losing control. She felt it building all over again, deeper and more intense with the swell of his maleness invading her, her muscles clenching at him to keep him hard and hot within her.

She felt the first tingle, and then the second before the avalanche hit her, stunning her with its totally devastating impact on her senses.

She felt Marc suddenly tense, the momentary stillness of his body heralding his subsequent cataclysmic plunge into paradise. She felt him empty himself inside her, the spilling warmth of his essence binding her to him in the most primal way imaginable.

She held him to her, relishing the feeling of him as close as could possibly be, the silence between them settling like breeze-driven blossoms falling softly to the ground.

She felt him move, the long stretch of his legs against hers reminding her of how intimately entwined she was, and not just physically. Her love for him seemed to fill every space in her body. She could barely take a breath without feeling it tug on her somewhere, a painful little tug that warned her that he did not care for her at all. His priority was Georgia and always would be.

She turned her head to look at him, the words of her confession already forming in her head, when she realised he was asleep.

'Marc?' She gave him a little shake.

There was no answer.

She gave a soft sigh and curled back into his warmth; she would tell him in the morning, but for tonight she would remain in his arms where she hoped with all her heart to stay for ever.

Nina knew something was terribly wrong as soon as she opened her eyes the next morning. The space beside her in the bed was empty and she could hear voices, urgent upset voices, echoing all through the villa. Her eyes went to the baby monitor but it showed no signs of being activated through the night.

She scrambled out of bed and threw on some clothes and rushed to Georgia's nursery where she found her niece just starting to wake, her tiny hands unfolding as she heard Nina come in. She gathered the baby close and turned around to see Paloma enter the room with a stricken expression.

'Whatever is the matter, Paloma?'

The Italian woman sank to a nearby chair, her face ashen. 'Signore Marcello passed away in his sleep last night. Marc is with him now.'

'Oh, no!' Nina cried.

'It has been expected for a long time but it is so sad,' Paloma said. 'For all his faults, all the staff members were very fond of him.'

'Is there anything I can do?'

Paloma gave her a sad smile. 'You have already made such a difference in the short time you have been here, *signora*. He died a happier, more peaceful man for having met his only grandchild.'

Nina found the next few days excruciatingly painful as she watched Marc deal with his grief over his father's passing whilst maintaining the family business and household affairs. Her plan to tell him of her deception was unthinkable now. He was barely able to cope with the stress of seeing to his father's funeral arrangements and the steady influx of calls of condolence from all over the world. She did what she could where she could, trying to take some of the burden from him, holding him in bed at night while he lost himself in her arms, again and again, as if their physical union was the only salve he could find to ease the sting of his loss. But during the day he often retreated into himself, reminding Nina of a lone wolf who trusted no one to come too close.

The day after the funeral Paloma informed her that Marc wished to speak with her in the study where he had been sorting through his father's papers.

He looked up as she came in, rising from the desk as she closed the door behind her. She was shocked at how tired he looked, his normally olive skin looked more sallow than tanned and his dark eyes had lines at the corners she hadn't noticed before.

'You wanted to see me, Marc?'

'I have been doing some thinking. I want to talk to you about Georgia's future.'

She felt her heart give a sudden lurch. Surely he wasn't thinking of a divorce so soon? Perhaps the death of his father had made him realise he could no longer tie himself in a loveless marriage indefinitely.

'W-what about her future?' she asked warily.

'I want to formally adopt Georgia.'

She swallowed, hunting for her voice, but when she found it she couldn't get it past the lump of panic in her throat.

'I want to be her father, not her uncle,' he went on. 'Nothing I can do will ever bring her real father back, and in time I will tell her about him, but for now I want to be her father in every way possible.'

Nina didn't know what to say. She saw the way Marc interacted with her niece, his dark eyes warm with deep affection as he cradled her in his arms or played with her, murmuring endearments to her in his own tongue. No one could question his ability to be a wonderful father, but she could hardly give the go-ahead for a formal adoption when she wasn't even the child's mother. And the thought of telling him now, after all he had been through...

'You don't seem all that enthusiastic,' he observed after a too long silence.

'I—I don't think it's such a good idea.'

'Why not?'

'No one can take Andre's place. He is her father even though he is no longer...here... I don't want to confuse her with you.'

'*Cristo*, Nina, I am doing everything a father would do. I am providing for her and protecting her. I do not see why she has to call me Uncle for the rest of her life when all I want is to be her father.'

'You are not her father.'

'Do you think I do not know that?'

She met his eyes briefly, trying to think of a reason to put him off. 'I don't trust you enough to let you take that step.'

He let out a sigh of exasperation. 'I married you, did I not? That's more than my brother did.'

'You only did it out of a sense of duty.'

'So what is wrong with that? Surely you were not expecting me to fall in love with you and promise you forever?'

Her eyes fell away from his. 'No, of course not, but I can't help thinking you have a hidden agenda. As soon as I let my guard slip you're going to snatch Georgia away from me. You've threatened me with it numerous times.'

He let out another deep sigh. 'I can understand your fears and I apologise for threatening you in such a way, but believe me, I had to ensure Georgia's safety. I had heard so much about you and I did not trust you to look after her in the way she needs.'

'What about now?' she asked, returning her gaze to his. 'Do you trust me now?'

He gave her a studied look before answering. 'My earlier misgivings have been somewhat resolved. However, I would be happier if I were officially documented as Georgia's father.'

'I'll think about it,' she said, buying for time.

'I suppose I will have to be satisfied with that for the time being, but I am warning you, Nina, I will not rest until I get what I want.'

Nina knew he meant every word. She saw it in the hard glitter of his eyes and the determined thrust of his chin. The only trouble was, she was in the way of him achieving his goal. He could never be Georgia's legal father, not unless he was to become fully aware of her deception. The web of lies she'd spun was threatening to choke her, each tiny gossamer thread pulling painfully on her heart as she thought about losing not only Georgia but Marc as well.

'There's something else I wish to tell you,' he said after a short tense silence. 'I have a business dinner tonight in Positano. I can't get out of it—there are people who wish to see me before I return to Sydney. I know it is short notice, but I would like you to come with me. Lucia will mind Georgia; I have already cleared it with her.'

Nina hesitated.

'Have you got something else planned?' he asked, his tone sharpening a fraction.

'No. No, of course not.'

'We will leave at seven. Wear something long; it is a formal affair.'

* * *

Lucia gave Nina an approving smile as she came down the stairs later that evening dressed in clinging black satin, her long hair twisted into a casual but stylish knot on top of her head, the escaping tendrils drifting over her cheeks giving her a softly sensual look.

'Will I do?' She twirled in front of the housekeeper.

'He will not be able to resist you tonight, Nina,' Lucia said.

Nina felt her cheeks heating and hastily covered her embarrassment by plucking at a tiny thread on her shoulder strap.

'You of all people know why he married me, Lucia.'

'Yes, but things have changed, have they not? You share his bed like a proper wife. That is good.'

Nina met the housekeeper's dark eyes. 'He doesn't love me. He hates me for what…for what I did to his brother.'

'But you didn't do anything to his brother, did you, Nina?' Lucia asked, her dark gaze never once leaving hers.

A tiny footstep of apprehension stepped on to a nerve in her spine. 'What do you mean?'

Lucia smiled a knowing smile. 'You might have fooled Signore Marcello but I am not so easily duped. It took me a few days to work it out but you are not Georgia's mother, are you?'

Nina's hand tightened a fraction on the banister. 'W-what makes you say that?'

'You could not possibly be the woman who seduced Andre.'

'W-why not?'

'Because I have met the woman you are pretending to be.'

Nina stared at her in shock, her hand falling away from the banister. *'You've met Nadia?'*

Lucia nodded. 'Yes. She came to the house to see Andre. I had stayed later than usual and ran into her. She was everything I had expected her to be: shallow and vain. She didn't even acknowledge me; I was just a nameless servant to her. Those first few days after you came I was confused. You acted like her, looked like her and even sounded like her. Then I had my suspicions, and when that phone call came and the voice sounded so like you I finally realised what was going on. I have twin sons myself. They are all grown up now but they often used to switch places for sheer devilment.'

Nina swallowed painfully. 'Have you told Marc?'

'No. I thought I would leave that to you.'

Nina caught her lip between her teeth for a moment.

'You have to tell him, you know,' Lucia said.

'I know.' She gave the housekeeper an agonised look. 'I just don't know how to do it. He has been through so much just lately…I didn't want to hurt him any more. I feel so guilty.'

'That guilt belongs to Nadia, not you. I suppose she left you with Georgia?'

'Yes. Believe me, it's the habit of a lifetime.' She gave a ragged sigh. 'Our mother was exactly the same: restless, moody, impulsive and irresponsible with a propensity to chase after totally unsuitable men.'

'He will understand,' Lucia assured her. 'He is a good man, Nina. He will be good to you once he knows who you really are.'

Nina wished she had her confidence. Somehow she didn't see Marc taking the news that well. No man liked to be made a fool of, and she had done that and more.

She heard the sound of his voice as he spoke to one of the staff as he came down the hall and she sent the housekeeper a tremulous smile as she tucked a strand of hair behind one ear. 'Wish me luck, Lucia.'

'Just be you, Nina,' Lucia advised. 'That is all you need to do.'

The dinner was held in a small but elegant hotel, the function room decked out with fragrant summer flowers and candelabra, the majority of the guests suited men with the occasional wife thrown in here and there. Nina had never felt less like socialising. She stayed close to Marc's side, her arm linked through his and smiled her way through the many introductions, but her heart wasn't in it and she couldn't wait for the night to be over.

After the meal was over a small band began to play and several couples got up to dance. Nina excused herself from the table and made her way to the ladies' room, more to escape the prospect of Marc's arms going around her on the dance floor than any other reason.

She locked herself in a cubicle and took several calming breaths, garnering up the courage for what she had to say to him as soon as they returned home.

She suddenly became aware of two women speaking just outside her cubicle, their voices rising above the sound of the hand dryer next to the basins. Though they spoke in Italian Nina was able to understand every damning word.

'I heard she was a topless dancer at a nightclub when his brother met her first. Apparently they had a hot affair for a while but then Andre Marcello decided he had better return to the respectability of his fiancée's arms.'

'I heard she'd had a baby,' another female voice said.

'Yes, rumour has it that's why Marc agreed to marry her. He wants his brother's child and marrying its mother was the only way to get it.'

'I hope he doesn't live to regret it. Women like Nadia Selbourne are trouble.'

'Apparently she goes by the name Nina now,' the other woman said with a little snicker. 'No doubt she wants to distance herself from her foray into blue movies. Apparently there was some other scandal that was hushed up too. Mind you, she has a great body considering she's not long had a baby. I wonder if Marc has been tempted to sample her for himself?'

'They're married, aren't they?'

Nina heard the cap of a lipstick tube being replaced.

'Marc Marcello is known to be highly selective in the women he chooses to sleep with,' the woman said. 'He only married her to get access to the child. But you know what they say about men: they don't think with their brains but what's between their legs.'

'I wouldn't mind having a look at what he's got between his legs,' the other woman said as they left the ladies' room.

Nina put her head in her hands and stifled a groan. Could it get any worse?

Marc rose when she came back to the table, his hand cupping her elbow. 'Would you like to dance?'

She wished she could think of an excuse but decided it was better to be on the dance floor with him than sitting at the table with the rest of the party who had heard God knew what else about her sister.

'All right,' she said. 'But I must warn you, I have two left feet.'

Marc led her to a less crowded corner of the dance floor and drew her closer, his chest brushing up against hers from time to time as he manoeuvred her around the other dancers.

'Andre told me you were a phenomenal dancer,' he said as he deftly turned her out of the way of another couple.

Nina quickly untied her feet. 'I don't know about that.' She sucked in a breath as he pulled her closer, her eyes skating away from his.

He frowned down at her. 'You have been on edge all evening. What is wrong? Are you worried about having to stay in Sorrento longer than we planned? I am sorry but there was nothing I could do. I have to tie up things here before we can return.'

She shook her head. 'No, it's not that.' She lifted her eyes to his, finally coming to a decision. 'Can we go home? I really need to talk to you—alone.'

He slid his hands down her arms and brought her closer. 'Is that what you want?'

'Yes.'

He turned her towards the table where his jacket and her bag were and, after a few brief farewells, escorted her towards the exit.

Marc barely spoke on the way home and Nina didn't know whether to be worried or grateful for his silence. She sat twisting her hands in her lap, pretending an interest in the passing view of twinkling lights in the distance. He pulled into the driveway a few minutes later and she waited until he came around to open her door, her heart thumping in apprehension as she got out.

'You looked very beautiful tonight,' he said, taking her hand as she got out of the car, his eyes holding hers as his thumb moved back and forth on the sensitive skin of her wrist.

'Marc...' She moistened her mouth, her throat closing over when his head came down, her breath stalling as his lips found hers.

His kiss was gentle at first, his hands light on her as he drew her even closer. Nina felt herself melting against him, her limbs loosening as his kiss became more insistent and his tongue more demanding as it mated sensually with hers.

Her hands found their way to his hair, her fingers burying in the black silk while her chest pushed against his with the urgency of her fast-growing need for more. She felt his hands at her breasts, shaping her, caressing her through the slippery fabric of her gown, the slide of silk over her tingling flesh an added delight to her highly tuned senses.

His groan as he pressed her back against the car stirred her into a frenzy of wanting. She ached for his hard thick presence and reached to touch him intimately, her fingers going to his waistband and releasing it to explore his jutting contours. He was hot and hard and heavy in her hands, his breathing becoming ragged as she explored him boldly.

His hand reached for the fall of her dress, sliding it up over her hips to bunch at her waist as his long fingers sought her liquid warmth. She gasped as he shifted the tiny lace panties out of his way, his fingers touching her tenderly but masterfully until she was breathless with the building sensations that were ricocheting through her.

She clung to him as he withdrew his fingers, replacing them with his solid length in one deep thrust that arched her backwards against the car. She felt her inner muscles clench him tightly, the shockwaves of delight coursing through her as he moved within her deeply and possessively, his building urgency inciting her own.

A cry burst from her lips as she neared the summit, her hips rocking with the motion of his to take her that final step. Her breath whooshed out of her when she finally made it, the earth-shattering feelings cascading through her veins like bubbles of champagne instead of blood. She felt light-headed and disconnected, her brain floating on a sea of pleasure, the receding tide washing over her in soft strokes like the lace of a foamy wave.

She opened her eyes to see the dark intensity of Marc's looking at her as he neared his own pinnacle of pleasure, his face contorted with the anticipation of rapidly approaching ecstasy. She held him as he shuddered against her, his body spilling into hers, his deeply muttered groans of release making her skin tingle with vicarious pleasure.

He was still breathing hard when he stepped back from her, his hands readjusting his trousers, his eyes still lit from behind as he held her gaze without speaking.

Nina smoothed down her gown and put a hand to her tumbling hair, her eyes falling away from his as she bent to retrieve the bag that had slipped to the floor at her feet.

His hand reached her bag first and they straightened together, Nina doing her best to appear unaffected by what had happened between them even though her legs were still shaking with reaction.

Marc tipped up her chin and forced her to look at him. 'Do not hide from me, Nina. I like to see the light of pleasure in your eyes.'

'I'm not hiding from you.' She took a breath and twisted out of his hold. 'Let's go inside. I feel cold.'

Marc let her go, following her into the house with a small frown etched between his brows.

Lucia was hovering in the foyer as soon as Nina opened the door, Marc just a few steps behind.

'What's wrong?' Nina asked, her blood running cold at the worried look on the housekeeper's face. 'Is Georgia all right?'

'Georgia is fine.' Lucia's hands twisted together as her eyes flicked towards the *salon* leading off the foyer.

'What is going on?' Marc asked as he closed the door behind him.

The housekeeper sent Nina an agonised look before turning to her employer. 'Signora Marcello has a visitor,' she announced.

Nina felt her colour drain away, her limbs going weak and her head swimming with panic.

'Who is it?' Marc asked as he shrugged himself out of his dinner jacket. 'Anyone I would know?'

There was a sound as the *salon* door opened and Marc looked up to see a mirror image of his wife framed in the doorway.

'Hello, Marc,' Nadia purred.

Nina felt the full force of Marc's dark eyes as they sought hers, his mouth a rigid line of incredulity, shock and unmistakable anger.

'Are you going to tell me what the hell is going on or am I supposed to guess?' His voice was razor-sharp.

Nina gave a convulsive swallow. 'I was going to tell you—'

Nadia stepped forward with a seductive sway of her hips, cutting her sister off mid-sentence. 'Isn't she a naughty little thing, Marc? Pretending to be me so she could get her hands on Georgia's inheritance.'

Nina gasped and grabbed Marc's arm to make him look at her. 'That's not true!'

He looked down at her hand on his sleeve, his expression one of distaste as he peeled it off, finger by finger.

He turned to his housekeeper and politely asked her to leave. Lucia gave Nina one last worried glance and made her way down the hall with slow steps that communicated her reluctance.

'Both of you.' Marc indicated the door of the *salon*. 'In here—now.'

Nadia sashayed her way back into the room, casting a sultry look over her shoulder at Marc as she did so.

Nina clenched her jaw and followed stiffly in her wake, her stomach twisting in despair.

Marc waited until the door was closed behind him before he spoke. 'Now, let us start from the beginning. Which of you is Georgia's mother?'

'I am.' Nadia stepped forward. 'I left her with Nina for a short period only to find she had stepped into my shoes while my back was turned.'

Nina's eyes flared in anger. 'I did no such thing! You abandoned her!'

'Don't listen to her.' Nadia's eyes glistened with ready tears. 'I love my daughter; she's all I have left of Andre. Nina was jealous. All she's ever wanted was to get married and have a baby. She tricked you into marrying her.'

'Marc!' Nina swung to face him. 'You mustn't listen to her! She's making it up!'

He looked at her for a brief moment before turning back to Nadia. 'I would like to speak to my…Nina alone for a moment. Will you excuse us?'

Nadia lifted her chin. 'She'll only tell more lies to cover her back. She did it for the money, you know. In spite of what she says, that's what she's after.'

Marc's hold on Nina's arm bit into her flesh as he led her out of the room, his face tight and his usually full mouth thin-lipped.

Nina didn't speak as he escorted her upstairs. She took one

look at the rage on his features and decided to wait until they were out of earshot of her twin.

Marc pushed open the door of his room and ushered her in, snapping it shut behind them.

His eyes hit hers—hard.

'You had better have a very good explanation for your behaviour or I swear to God you will wish you had never been born.'

'I was going to tell you—'

'When?' he barked at her. 'When were you going to tell me you had deceived me in such a despicable way?'

'I didn't do it deliberately—' she began.

'Do not lie to me!' he shouted. 'You played me for a fool from the start.' He shoved a hand through his hair and stepped away from her, shaking his head in disbelief. 'I cannot believe you would stoop so low.' He turned back to glare at her. 'Was it worth it? Did you have a good laugh behind my back at how you had tricked me?'

'No! I—'

'Damn you, Nina,' he ground out darkly as he came towards her, his hands clenched by his sides. 'You made a fool out of me and that I will not forgive.'

'Marc...please let me explain.' She twisted her hands in front of her in agitation. 'I didn't mean it to go this far. When you arrived at my flat that day I was so concerned you were going to take Georgia away. I had to do something! I didn't know it would lead to this, I swear I didn't.'

'Why did you not come clean when you had the chance?' he asked. 'You have strung me along with a web of lies the whole time. You have had numerous opportunities to tell me and yet you did not.'

'I know! I'm sorry...I was frightened. I thought you wouldn't let me see Georgia any more. You kept threatening to take her away; I had no choice.'

He gave a disgusted sound at the back of his throat and

turned away from her. 'You must think me the biggest fool, but don't forget I know that as soon as that money was put in your account you spent it.'

'I didn't spend it! I gave it to Nadia as she insist—'

'You cooked this up together, did you not?' His eyes grew dark and dangerous.

'What?' She looked at him in bewilderment.

He gave a cynical snort. 'I can see what you have been up to. The twin routine is an old one but effective if played well. And you certainly played it very well, very well indeed. You switched personalities with the blink of an eye.'

'I'm not proud of what I did but I—'

His venomous look cut her off. 'Was it fun, Nina? Was it fun making a fool out of me? Did you enjoy yourself? Did you get off on the fact that I could not help myself, that I slept with you in spite of my determination not to?'

'I never intended sleeping with you. You have to believe that.'

'I believe nothing of what you say!' he spat. 'How can I, after all you have done?'

'I didn't mean to hurt you.'

'Hurt me?' He gave her an imperious look. 'You would have to try much harder, Nina, if you wanted to hurt me. I am well used to the perfidious nature of women like you and know how to protect myself.' He swung away to open the door, indicating he was finished with her. 'I will give you until midday tomorrow to get out of my house. I will send the divorce papers to you as soon as you provide me with a forwarding address.'

Nina stared at him, shock rendering her immobile, her legs refusing to take her even one step forward.

'Did you not hear me?' he asked.

'I want to see Georgia regularly,' she said, trying to keep the tears back.

A tiny nerve pulsed at the corner of his mouth. 'That will depend entirely on her mother.'

'Nadia doesn't care for Georgia. She only cares for herself. She abused her. I know it for a fact. And she'll do it again just as our mother did.'

'Your sister is Georgia's mother and therefore her legal guardian. You have no say in what happens to her.'

'Nor do you,' she pointed out.

'Your sister and I will no doubt come to some mutually satisfying arrangement.'

'As long as there is plenty of money involved, Nadia will be very satisfied,' she said bitterly. 'But you should think twice before you leave her alone with Georgia. She is not to be trusted.'

'And you think you have the market cornered on trust?' he sneered. 'You, who lied to me every time you could? Why should I believe a single word you say?'

'I wanted what was best for Georgia. That was my only motivation. I don't care if you don't believe me; you can't make it untrue just by not believing what I say.'

He gave her a brittle look. 'I would prefer it if I did not have to see you again. I will arrange for a car to take you to the airport tomorrow but as far as I am concerned I never want to set eyes on you again.'

Nina knew she was beaten. She saw it in the hard glitter of his eyes and in the tight set of his mouth. Hatred seeped from every pore of his body towards her, stinging her in its intensity.

She stalked past him, refusing to allow him to see how broken she really was. She kept her expression blank, her shoulders straight and her head at a devil-may-care angle.

She made it to her room just in time, the tears flowing from so deep inside her she couldn't stem the flow. She lay face down on the bed and sobbed until her throat was raw and her eyes swollen. After a few minutes she dragged herself up and, stuffing what she could into a small bag, hoisted it over her shoulder. She crept into Georgia's room and stood looking down at her for a few heart-wrenching moments.

She touched the baby's petal-like cheek with her fingers. 'Goodbye, darling, I will never forget you as long as I live. I'd do anything to keep you, but Marc...' She bit her lip. 'Marc doesn't want me.' She choked back a sob and continued. 'He loves you, sweetie. He loves you a lot. I know he will be a wonderful father to you. I know that with every beat of my heart.'

Nina closed the door softly and made her way down the stairs and, with barely a sound, walked out of the house and out of Marc's life as if she had never been.

Marc had returned to the *salon*, where Nadia Selbourne was helping herself to a large tumbler of his best brandy. She gave him a seductive smile and raised her glass in a toast as he came in.

'Sorted out everything, Marc? Did she confess?'

He compressed his lips and ran a hand through his hair in a distracted manner without answering.

'She's always been jealous of me, you know,' Nadia continued. 'I've always been the one with the boyfriends but no one takes a second look at her because she's too shy. Pathetic, don't you think? I mean she's still a bloody virgin, unless you've dealt with that. At twenty-four! Can you believe it?'

Marc froze.

Nadia sat down and crossed her long legs, her eyes running over him speculatively. 'I take it you want to keep Georgia?'

He finally located his voice. 'Yes.'

She gave him a look from beneath her lashes, the glass in her hand making a slight ringing noise as she ran her fingertip around the rim. 'I can't give her what you can give her.' She made a little moue with her lips. 'But if you want to adopt her...well...' She gave a streetwise smile. 'I won't stand in your way if the price is right, so to speak.'

Marc forced himself to concentrate on what she was saying, even though his mind was flying off at disturbing tangents.

'Name your price.'

She named a figure that would have shocked him under any other circumstances.

'I'll have the legal papers drawn up in the morning,' he said.

Nadia uncrossed then re-crossed her legs, a little smile still playing about her mouth. 'Why not give me an advance right now? I need to find somewhere to stay—unless you have a bed I could use?'

Marc ground his teeth behind his cool polite smile. 'How much?' he asked, reaching for his wallet.

She got up from the sofa and floated over to him, her talon-tipped fingers taking the wad of notes he held out to her. 'You know…' She tiptoed her fingertips up the front of his shirt. 'You are so much nicer than your brother. He wouldn't give me anything in the end.'

Marc removed her hand. 'He gave you a child.'

She gave another pout. 'I never wanted her. I only went through with it because Nina insisted.'

Marc fought with himself not to physically throw her out. He couldn't believe how two sisters, and twins at that, could be so different. Nadia was everything Nina was not. And, fool that he was, he hadn't realised it till now.

'I will call you a cab,' he said, moving towards the phone.

'Are you sure you don't want me to stay and keep you company?' She gave him a little wink as she slid a hand down her hip in a seductive manner.

'No.' He held the door open for her. 'I will see you out.'

Once Nadia had left, Marc went upstairs in search of Nina, his apology already rehearsed in his head. How could he have got it so wrong? Of course Nina would have done whatever she could to protect Georgia—including marrying a man she didn't know—rather than allow her niece to suffer being brought up by a totally selfish mother.

How had he not guessed? She was nothing like Nadia. She

was loyal and devoted, selfless and shy, and—he gave a painful swallow—she had been a virgin.

'Nina?' He knocked at her door but there was no answer. He opened it but it was empty except for a few scattered articles of clothing suggesting she had packed in a hurry, not bothering to take everything with her.

'Nina!' He called out louder as he went through to the nursery, the door swinging back against the wall in his haste.

Georgia awoke with a start and immediately began crying, her tiny frightened sobs galvanizing him out of his temporary stasis.

'Hey there, little one,' he soothed as he picked her up, holding her over his shoulder, stroking her as he made his way back through the rest of the villa in search of Nina.

Georgia was inconsolable, her cries growing louder and more frantic, as if she sensed the panic coming off him in waves.

'Do not cry,' he pleaded as he searched the downstairs rooms. 'We will find her, do not worry. We *have* to find her.'

After twenty minutes he knew he was beaten. Nina was gone and he was left holding the baby—a very unhappy baby who was crying out for the mother she had come to know as her own.

CHAPTER FIFTEEN

NINA decided against using the airport at Naples and hailed a cab to take her to Rome instead. She took the first available flight, arriving in Sydney bleary-eyed and broken-hearted. She stayed with Elizabeth for a week, hardly coming out of her room, her eyes red from bouts of weeping, her slim build visibly shrinking as each day passed.

Elizabeth sat on the end of her bed on the seventh day and frowned in concern. 'Come on, Nina. Don't take this lying down. Go and see him and tell him how you feel. Yesterday's paper said he's back in town now.'

'I can't,' Nina sobbed.

'Yes, you can,' her friend insisted. 'You love him and you love Georgia. He needs to know.'

'He hates me.'

'How do you know that? Things might have changed by now. Who knows? A full dose of Nadia might have set him straight.'

Nina rolled on to her back and scrubbed at her eyes. 'It's my fault for not telling him the truth from the start. He has every right to be angry. He married the wrong woman.'

'What rubbish!' Elizabeth said. 'He married the right one, if you ask me. You are everything he needs. You are loyal and faithful and would rather suffer yourself than hurt someone else. What more could a man ask for?'

Nina's chin wobbled. 'I just wish I could tell him how I feel.'

Elizabeth got to her feet. 'Do it.' She handed her the phone from the bedside table. 'Call him now and ask to see him.'

Nina stared at the phone for a long moment.

'Go on,' she urged. 'What's his number and I'll dial it for you.'

Nina took the phone with an unsteady hand. 'No…no, I'll call him.'

'Good girl.' Elizabeth gave her an encouraging smile. 'I'll leave you to it.' She went to the door and turned back to add, 'Good luck.'

Nina gave her a tremulous smile and, although she'd only said she'd call Marc to get her friend off her back, she looked down at the phone in her hands, surprised to see she had pressed more than half the numbers in already. She took a shaky breath and pressed the last three.

'Nina?' Lucia answered on the second ring. *'Dio!* Where are you? We have been so worried! Georgia is not sleeping and Marc is—'

'Is she all right?' Nina gasped.

'She is missing her mother,' Lucia said.

'Where is Nadia?'

Lucia made a noise of disgust in the back of her throat. 'Not that mother—you. Your sister took the money and left.'

'What money?'

'The money she asked for in exchange for Georgia,' Lucia informed her.

Nina closed her eyes. 'And…Marc? How…how is he?'

'He is angry.'

'I know.' Nina bit her lip. 'I don't blame him.'

'Where are you?' Lucia asked. 'He will want to see you.'

'He told me he never wanted to see me again.'

'That was then, this is now. Come around tonight. I will take Georgia home with me so you can have the evening together to sort things out.'

'I don't know if it can be sorted out.'

'Just come home, Nina. This is where you belong.'

Nina was sitting on the edge of the sofa in Marc's house when she heard his car come up the drive. She'd spent an hour with Georgia before Lucia had taken her with her, the baby settling as if by magic as soon as Nina tucked her into the baby seat in the back of the housekeeper's car.

She heard Marc swear as he entered the house, the rough expletive cutting through the air like a knife. She rose to her feet as the lounge room door was pushed open, her hands in a tight knot in front of her body, her eyes hesitantly searching for his.

He came to a complete halt as his eyes met hers, his colour draining away as if he'd just been given the shock of his life.

'Nina?' He stepped towards her, then stopped. 'It is you?'

'Yes, it's me.'

'I was not sure…' He pushed a hand through his hair, making it even more untidy than it already was. 'I was expecting your sister. She called today, asking for more money.'

'What did you say to her?'

He gave her a quick glance before looking away. 'There is not much I can say until the adoption papers are processed.'

'She's letting you adopt Georgia?'

'Yes, for a price, of course.'

'Of course.'

He met her eyes once more, his expression guarded. 'Why are you here?'

'I wanted to see Georgia.'

He held her gaze for an interminable second or two. 'Is that all?'

'No.' She took another breath and added softly, 'I wanted to see you.'

'Why?' His one word held a note of accusation as if he thought she too was after his money.

'I wanted to tell you that I'm sorry for what I did. I thought I was doing the best thing for Georgia but…I can see now how terribly wrong it was. I thought you would take her away from me but I know you are not the hard man you pretend to be. You are…' She tripped over a little sob. 'You are the most wonderful man I have ever met.'

'You are her mother in ways your sister could never be,' he said, his voice suddenly rough with emotion. 'I was wrong to speak to you the way I did. I was so angry at how you had deceived me. I never once stopped to think of what you had sacrificed in order to protect Georgia from Nadia.'

'W-what do you mean?'

A shadow of a smile haunted his mouth. 'You gave yourself to me. I had no idea what you were doing at the time. I simply assumed you had had a difficult birth with Georgia, never once suspecting that not only were you not her mother but that you were also a virgin.'

Colour seeped into her cheeks and she had to look away.

'No.' He stepped towards her, taking her by the shoulders in a gentle hold so she had no choice but to meet his eyes. 'Do not hide the truth from me any longer. You gave yourself to me and I want to know why.'

'I…' Her eyes fell away from his. 'I couldn't help it. I had never felt that way before.' She lifted her eyes back to his. 'I think I fell in love with you that first day when you came to my flat. You picked up Georgia and you had tears in your eyes. I know you were grieving the loss of your brother but you still had room for her in your heart and were prepared to do anything to protect her. I had the very same feelings. It made me realise we were more alike than different. I couldn't help falling in love with you.'

He swallowed convulsively as he reached for her, burying his head into her neck. 'I have wronged you so abominably. How can you love me?'

She felt the moisture of his eyes against her skin and hugged him tightly. 'I just do. No rhyme or reason. I just do.'

He pulled back from her, his expression tortured. 'I cannot believe I am hearing this. You mean you forgive me for what I said to you?'

'You were angry.'

'Not just angry,' he admitted ruefully. 'I was so hurt. I imagined you laughing behind my back at how you had hoodwinked me.'

She gave him a quizzical look. 'I thought you said you never allowed yourself to get hurt?'

He smiled. 'You are not the only one who can tell lies, you know. Of course I was hurt. In spite of what I believed to be true of you, I had fallen in love with you. I wanted to believe you were not capable of the behaviour that had led to my brother's death, but every now and again you would remind me of it by acting like your sister. I had no choice but to think you were one and the same.'

'And yet you fell in love with me?'

He gathered her closer. 'How could I not? You were always so loving towards Georgia and you responded to me so delightfully. I ached for you day and night and, while I hated myself for my weakness, there was nothing I could do to stop myself from touching you.'

She sighed against the solid warmth of his chest. 'I can't believe you love me.'

He stroked a hand through her hair, pressing her to his heart. 'You had better believe it. I have been out of my mind these last few days trying to find you. I have not slept or eaten in days.'

She smiled up at him. 'Me neither. I missed you so much.'

He gave her a suddenly serious look. 'I have lain awake at night agonising over the ways I have insulted you. Do you know how wretched I feel? You are the most beautiful person, your nature is gentle and loving and your natural shyness so endearing. I have been such a fool for not seeing it from the first. If I had been thinking clearly I would have, but I was torn apart by Andre's death and my father's demands to claim Georgia no matter what the cost. I knew he was dying, time was running out and I had to do whatever I could to fulfil his last wish.'

Nina stroked his jaw tenderly, her eyes shining with moisture. 'Don't be so hard on yourself. I was the one in the wrong. I should have told you right at the beginning when you came to my flat but I was frightened you'd take Georgia away. I didn't think. I just acted on impulse and then it was too late to back out.'

'I railroaded you, *cara*,' he said with regret. 'I can see that now. I was determined to show you for the money-hungry opportunist I believed you to be. I didn't allow for any other explanation.'

'But it's over now,' she said. 'We have each other and we have Georgia.'

'But you have been cheated out of so many things.' His expression turned serious again. 'A proper church wedding, for one thing, and a honeymoon. I do not know how I am going to even begin to make it up to you.'

She gave him a twinkling smile and nestled close. 'I don't mind so much about the wedding but I do mind about the honeymoon. How soon can we go on one?'

Marc smiled as he scooped her up in his arms and carried her towards the door. 'How about now?'

HARLEQUIN *Presents*

Passion and Seduction Guaranteed!

She's sexy, successful and pregnant!

Relax and enjoy our fabulous
series about couples whose
passion results in pregnancies...
sometimes unexpected!

Share the surprises, emotions, drama and suspense
as our parents-to-be come to terms with the prospect
of bringing a new life into the world. All will discover
that the business of making babies brings with it
the most special joy of all....

February's Arrival:

PREGNANT BY THE MILLIONAIRE

by Carole Mortimer

What happens when Hebe Johnson finds out she's
pregnant with her noncommittal boss's baby?

Find out when you buy
your copy of this title today!

REQUEST YOUR FREE BOOKS!

HARLEQUIN® *Presents*~®

**2 FREE NOVELS
PLUS 2
FREE GIFTS!**

*PASSION
GUARANTEED
SEDUCTION*

YES! Please send me 2 FREE Harlequin Presents® novels and my 2 FREE gifts. After receiving them, if I don't wish to receive any more books, I can return the shipping statement marked "cancel." If I don't cancel, I will receive 6 brand-new novels every month and be billed just $3.80 per book in the U.S., or $4.47 per book in Canada, plus 25¢ shipping and handling per book and applicable taxes, if any*. That's a savings of close to 15% off the cover price! I understand that accepting the 2 free books and gifts places me under no obligation to buy anything. I can always return a shipment and cancel at any time. Even if I never buy another book from Harlequin, the two free books and gifts are mine to keep forever.

106 HDN EEXK 306 HDN EEXV

Name _____ (PLEASE PRINT) _____

Address _____ Apt. # _____

City _____ State/Prov. _____ Zip/Postal Code ____

Signature (if under 18, a parent or guardian must sign) _____

Mail to the Harlequin Reader Service®:

IN U.S.A.
P.O. Box 1867
Buffalo, NY
14240-1867

IN CANADA
P.O. Box 609
Fort Erie, Ontario
L2A 5X3

Not valid to current Harlequin Presents subscribers.

Want to try two free books from another line?
Call 1-800-873-8635 or visit www.morefreebooks.com.

* Terms and prices subject to change without notice. NY residents add applicable sales tax. Canadian residents will be charged applicable provincial taxes and GST. This offer is limited to one order per household. All orders subject to approval. Credit or debit balances in a customer's account(s) may be offset by any other outstanding balance owed by or to the customer. Please allow 4 to 6 weeks for delivery.

HP06

They're tall, dark…and ready to marry!

If you love reading about our sensual Italian men, don't delay—look out for the next story in this great miniseries!

THE ITALIAN'S FORCED BRIDE
by Kate Walker

Alice knew Domenico would never love her back—so she left him. Now he is demanding that she return to his bed. And when he finds out she's pregnant, he might never let her go….

Available this February.

Also from this miniseries, coming up in April:
SICILIAN HUSBAND, BLACKMAILED BRIDE
by Kate Walker

HARLEQUIN *Presents*

If you love strong, commanding men—
you'll love this miniseries...

RUTHLESS

Men who can't be tamed...or so they think!

THE SICILIAN'S MARRIAGE ARRANGEMENT
by Lucy Monroe

Hope is overjoyed when sexy Sicilian tycoon Luciano
proposes marriage. Hope is completely in love with
her gorgeous husband—until Luciano confesses
he had had no choice but to wed her....

On sale in February...buy yours today!

Brought to you by your favorite Harlequin Presents authors!

Coming in March:

WANTED: MISTRESS AND MOTHER
by Carol Marinelli,
Book #2616
